Journey Through The Night

BOOK III

Dawn's Early Light

D1611761

Journey Through The Night

BOOK III

Dawn's Early Light

by

Anne De Vries

INHERITANCE PUBLICATIONS
NEERLANDIA, ALBERTA, CANADA
PELLA, IOWA, U.S.A.

National Library of Canada Cataloguing in Publication Data
Vries, Anne de, 1904-1964.
 Journey through the night

 Translation of: Reis door de nacht.
 ISBN 0-921100-25-6

  1. Netherlands—History—German occupation, 1940-1945—Fiction.
 2. World War, 1939-1945—Netherlands—Fiction. I.Title.
 PT5878.V57R413 2001   839.3'1362   C2001-910236-4

Library of Congress Cataloging-in-Publication Data
Vries, Anne de, 1904-1964
  [Reis door de nacht. English]
  Journey through the night / by Anne De Vries ; [translated by Harry
 der Nederlanden].
  373 p. : ill. ; 23 cm.
   ISBN 0-921100-25-6 (pbk)
   1. Netherlands—History—German occupation, 1940-1945—Fiction.
 I.Nederlanden, Harry der. II. Title.
 PT5878.V57 R413 2001
 839.3'1362—dc21
 2001000785

ISBN 9780921100256 (all 4 volumes in one)
5th Printing (in individual volumes) 2014, 2018.
978-1-928136-38-5 Book I - Into the Darkness
978-1-928136-39-2 Book II - The Darkness Deepens
978-1-928136-40-8 Book III - Dawn's Early Light
978-1-928136-41-5 Book IV - A New Day

Originally published as *Reis door de Nacht. A New Day*
by Uitgeverij G.F. Callenbach B.V., Nijkerk, The Netherlands
Published with permission.

Translated by Harry der Nederlanden

Cover Painting by Reint De Jonge
Illustrated by Tjeerd Bottema

Published simultaneously in the U.S.A. by Inheritance Publications
Box 366, Pella, Iowa 50219

Printed in the U.S.A.

CHAPTER ONE

John sat at the table near the window, but the curtain was drawn. Chin in his hands, he yawned. Uncle Herman was at school, and Aunt Haddie was gone for the afternoon, doing her shopping. She shopped in the east end of town because she knew a grocer there. Sometimes he would let her have a few pounds of potatoes without a ration card. That was worth the long walk. Then she would walk to another side of town where a store carried a new kind of imitation coffee that was supposed to taste just like the real thing. She would probably have to stand in line for a long time at both stores. So John had the house to himself for the afternoon.

First he had washed the dishes and swept the floor, and then he had done a few exercises — very carefully, of course. The neighbours, who had seen his uncle and aunt leave, must not notice that someone was still at home. Next he had checked the calendar to find out which phase of the moon it was, for Uncle Herman allowed him to go outside only on nights when it was very dark. But it was only the first quarter; he would have to wait more than a week, unless it clouded over. He could better be in jail. At least there he would get a little fresh air every day.

He had been sitting over his books for almost an hour now, but he couldn't keep his mind on his studies. It seemed so aimless, this studying without any specific goal or direction.

Pensively he looked through the curtain and into the street. Look, across the street was a party man, a member of the National Socialist Movement (N.S.M.). In his flashy new suit, he was on his way to work in one of the bureaucracies created by the occupation government. He also had a brand-new bike, the parasite! He probably greased a few palms to get it.

The opportunist leaned the glittering new machine against the wall and went back to lock his door. He turned and stood on the doorstep for a moment, surveying the block like a baron viewing his domain. He grinned as a man in patched overalls went rattling by on a bike with wooden tires. Then Dapper Dan wheeled his precious bicycle off the sidewalk and slid onto the seat. Sure, go ahead, look at this window — you can't see me anyway! But if you did, you little bureaucrat, would you turn me in for thirty guilders? Or would you do it for nothing?

What time was it by now? Almost three o'clock. About time for that cigarette-butt collector to come by again; he never missed a day. He seemed to have a fixed route . . . Sure enough, there he was, right on schedule. You would think a big strong man like that would have a job somewhere. But, who knows, maybe he makes more money this way, takes the butts home every night, peels off the paper and then mixes the tobacco with plenty of peat or chopped cherry leaves. And then he sells the concoction on the black market under some fancy new name.

The collector bent down twice on the block to put something in his pocket. What people won't do for a smoke! Sometimes Uncle Herman smoked some ersatz tobacco in his pipe. It stank up the whole house, smelling like a smoldering dust rag. But he had planted his little ten by ten garden full of tobacco plants, and he tended them much more lovingly than he had ever tended his flowers. When they were liberated . . . If they ever were liberated . . .

The longer John was cooped up, the more pessimistic he became. In Italy and Northern Africa, the Germans had surrendered in mid-May. But Italy and Africa were a long way from Holland. And since that time the Allies had made little headway. The much-touted spring offensive that the Germans were supposed to launch in Russia seemed to have fizzled. They were even losing ground. But everything seemed to be going so slowly! And where was the invasion? Supposedly it had been in the works for a couple of years already. Or was it all just so much talk? Why didn't the English and the Americans come through with that tremendous force of planes, warships, and troops that Radio Orange kept praising? Were they waiting until the Germans had fortified the whole European coast from Spain to Norway?

The construction of the Western Coastline was well underway. Soon massive concrete pillboxes and barbed-wire barriers would line the whole coast. The long pier in Scheveningen had been dismantled, and most of the houses along the beaches had been destroyed. Thousands of people had been forced to evacuate to other parts of the country, including Uncle Herman and Aunt Haddie. They had been assigned to a small, isolated village, where they were to be housed in a farmer's tool shed.

But Uncle Herman had been fortunate enough to get a teaching position in Amsterdam, and after living in a boarding house for two months, he had been given this townhouse. At one time it had been occupied by a Jewish family, but they had been among the first to be deported to the concentration camp at Westerbork. Now the townhouse was John's refuge and his prison. How long would he have to stay here? There was no end in sight.

He sighed, took his wallet out of his pocket, and studied a photograph. A pretty girl in a nurse's uniform looked back at him, eyes sparkling with good humour. Rita. What a girl! Whenever he got depressed, he could take one look at the picture and find new heart. If he looked at the picture enough, she would almost seem to begin talking to him. "Don't give up, John," she would say. "It's rough now, but it won't last forever. I love you. And one day . . ."

He turned to the next photograph. The countryside, and a white house nestled among fruit trees. Standing in front of it, his whole family: Father, Mother, himself, Fritz, Tricia, Hanneke, Trudy, little Hansie, and an old man with a rake — Uncle Gerrit. What a beautiful house it had been! Was it only two months ago that they had still been living there all together? It seemed like much, much longer. They might still be living together peacefully as a family if — yes, he might as well say it — if Father had paid no attention to the war, carrying on as usual, like Uncle Herman.

But not Father! He couldn't bear to see injustice done and not try to change things. Nor could he close his door to people in trouble. And before they knew it, the whole family had been up to their ears in the resistance movement, spreading illegal newspapers, taking in divers, hiding English fliers, helping Jews. Still, everything had been going fine until Wallinga, their Nazi neighbour, had betrayed them.

John remembered every detail of that day as vividly as if it had been yesterday. At the end of the general strike, Father had called in all the local resistance workers to discuss the explosive situation. Seeing all the bikes, Wallinga had tipped off the Germans. If they hadn't been warned just in time, they would all have been sitting in a German concentration camp by now. Or worse!

Closing his eyes, John relived those awful moments. Pulling his sister Hanneke along with one hand and Marie, their little Jewish refugee, with the other, he had raced through the orchard into the woods. In the pine trees he had stopped to wait for the others. He was calm, and yet fear lodged in his chest like a bullet in his breastbone. William, a medical student who had been living with them, rushed by to warn the

Liebstadts, a Jewish family living in the woods in a camper.

Then came Tricia, carrying Hansie, and right on her heels was Mother, with an armload of sheets that she had yanked from the clothesline. Fritz came puffing up with Trudy on his back. Last of all came Father, holding a big, blue revolver in his hand. He took Marie's hand and shouted at John to keep going.

Looking back, John caught a glimpse of a big, gray truck pulling into the yard. Then he was in the trees. Towing Hanneke behind him, he ran down the winding trail. Suddenly Hanneke began to wail. Quickly he picked her up and carried her, his hand over her mouth. Soon they caught up with William and the Liebstadts. The old man needed help, so John took Marie again, and Father helped Mr. Liebstadt. Behind them they heard a shot and some muffled shouting, and then a hail of gunfire. After that, the shooting didn't stop. Uncle Gerrit and David, the American pilot, must have started a gunfight to give them more time to escape. The diversion worked! Single file they sneaked through wheat fields and cornfields, following windbreaks and hedges until they got to the Hoving farm, where they hid in the barn. In the distance they saw the smoke of the burning house rising above the pines.

But they wouldn't be safe at the Hovings, for the Germans could easily track them down with dogs. Soon they all climbed aboard a farm wagon, covered themselves with straw, and Hoving drove them to another town, there they were taken in by one of the local ministers. They got the news from home that same night: the house had burned to the ground and David was dead. His body had been found in the ashes.

The Germans were furious; one soldier had been killed and another critically wounded. A third had caught a bullet in the shoulder. Wallinga, too, had been killed — paid on the spot for his act of betrayal. German reinforcements had arrived from town, and within a few hours they had begun to search all the homes in the vicinity. Nothing was known of Uncle Gerrit. Apparently he had burned with the house.

But in the middle of the night, someone tapped softly on the parsonage window and whistled the first line of the national anthem. When they opened the door, there was Uncle Gerrit. He had minor burns on his face and

hands, but he was very happy to see the whole family safe. He had managed to escape through the tunnel he had built for David. Yes, David had burned with the house, but he had been dead already — killed by a German bullet.

The next day Uncle Gerrit went back to the burnt house to look after the orchard and the animals. The garage and his little apartment above the garage were still intact. No one would suspect that he had been the one doing the shooting, and he would be clever enough to lead the Germans around by the nose.

In the next few days, the family had been separated and sent to different addresses. Now they were the homeless wanderers. They had shown hospitality to many people; now they would have to depend on the hospitality of others. Father and John were warned that their pictures would appear in the police bulletin; they would be sought as terrorists and killers. Their apprehension and arrest had been given high priority; therefore, it was unsafe for them to stay anywhere near their hometown.

Van der Mey, a policeman who worked for the underground, took them to Zwolle in his car. William went along as far as Meppel, where he hoped to stay with friends. John and Father had caught a train to Amsterdam and had arrived safely at Uncle Herman and Aunt Haddie's. Uncle Herman could hardly refuse to shelter his nephew, but he laid down two ground rules: John was to have nothing to do with "that underground foolishness," and he was never to set foot outside the apartment without his uncle's permission. John had no choice but to agree. Besides, after everything that had happened, he'd had a bellyful of underground work.

That had been almost two months ago, and all that time he hadn't seen any of the family. Rita had made two trips from Rotterdam to see him. Those had been wonderful days! Every once in a while he got a letter from Mother, mailed to him by Van der Mey. And he could also write back to her in care of Van der Mey. She was still living in the parsonage with the two youngest children, but she had no idea where he and Father were hiding. That way, if she were found by the Germans, she could truthfully say that she knew nothing of the whereabouts of her son and husband.

He wrote to Father in care of the same address, but Father wrote back directly, once from Zwolle and another time from Utrecht. So Father had no fixed address; he must be staying active in resistance work. If Father could do it, why not he? Here he was just wasting time.

John had been ready for his high school final exams, but now he wouldn't be able to take them. He was studying history; it had always been his favourite subject, and once he had intended to major in it in college. But he was just plodding along now. How could he concentrate on the ancient Greeks and the Persian Wars when the whole modern world was being turned into rubble?

"You've done your share," Uncle Herman had told him. But was that true? Had you ever done your share? Sitting here, he had only a faint idea how the war was going. After the general strike in May, all the people had been ordered to turn in their radios. Although Uncle Herman hadn't turned his in, he had been too frightened to keep it in the house, so he had wrapped it up and buried it in the garden. The daily newspapers carried only what the Nazis wanted the people to read — lies, mostly. And the reports that Uncle Herman brought home from school — how much of those could you believe? The city was full of rumours.

But recently someone had been dropping an underground newspaper into the mailbox — a newspaper that John had never seen before. *True* was its name. A few times he had managed to get it before Uncle Herman could destroy it. He had put those issues in his hiding place up in the attic behind a couple of rafters, and sometimes he went up there to read them through once more. Then, for a while, he would feel one with his friends in the resistance, that anonymous army of men who, although they didn't know each other, were united in their struggle.

But now he had been forced to drop out of that army, maybe forever. He was like a soldier who had been knocked out of action.

He sighed and tried to get his mind back on his book.

Ring-ring-ring-rrring! Someone was at the door! Three shorts and one long — the first measure of Beethoven's Fifth Symphony and Morse code for "V," or victory!

He jumped up, his heart pounding. This was the first time in his two months here that he had heard that signal. Who could it be? The signal meant that the caller was sound. Or was it a trick to get him to the door?

He slid to the floor, crawled under the table to the other side of the window, and peeked outside from behind the curtain. Ring-ring-ring-rrring! The same signal. At the door with his back to the window stood a man with a briefcase under his arm. He was wearing a neat gray suit. But there was something familiar about him. John moved the curtain, and now he could see the red hair. Of course! He sprinted across the room, skidded down the hall, and threw open the door.

"William!" he shouted jubilantly.

"Hi, John. Surprise!"

John embraced him and pulled him into the hallway. They pounded each other's shoulders and jabbed each other in the ribs. One minute he had been miserable and feeling sorry for himself, and now — here was his best friend! He could hardly believe his eyes.

"You ugly redhead, you're still as mean as ever!" said John, laughing delightedly. "You haven't changed a bit!"

"But *you* sure have," said William. "You're as skinny as a rail. Look, I've skinned my knuckles on your bony ribs. Have you been sick or something?"

"No, that comes from living on city rations," said John, grinning. "Come on, let's go into the living room. And keep your voice down, or else the neighbours will think there's a diver hiding here. Sit down! Sorry I can't offer you any coffee, but I just . . ."

As always, William liked to play the role of the rich uncle. Putting on a beneficent face, he opened his briefcase and lined up two chocolate bars on the table. "One for you, and one for me," he said. "Share and share alike — that's how it will be from now on."

"Where did you get them?"

"Don't ask," said William. "To our reunion! How's it going? Yes, I know. But at least you're alive and kicking. But you can kiss these four walls goodbye. You're coming with me!"

"You're kidding!" John felt the blood rushing to his face.

"No, really!"

"But . . . but I'm not supposed to show my face on the street."

"Nonsense. Lots of people saw your face on your way down here, didn't they?"

"But they're *looking* for me. You know that. My picture has been in the police bulletin!"

"So what? They're looking for me, too. And my picture has been in the police bulletin too, red hair and all. What do you think? That every policeman is walking around with your picture in his pocket? The Germans have pictures out on half the population. There's no way the police can keep track of all those faces. Sure, if you're picked up for something, there's a chance they might recognize you from their files. But we're not going to do anything dumb and get picked up, are we? You've got a good I.D., I hope? What's your occupation at the moment?"

"Teacher. See, here's . . ."

"So, you stole my job, eh? Well, I've become a railway inspector. A much better job! I get to ride free anywhere in the country. Really! Just take a look. What's the name of your school?"

"What?"

"Well, if you're a teacher, you've got to teach somewhere."

"Oh, right! Let's see . . . Let's say I teach at the Abraham Kuyper School."

"No, not 'let's say' — you're either at the Abraham Kuyper School or you're not. You teach the third grade, your principal's name is Mr. Jansen, and you have the room at the end of the hall. And when you're travelling with me, your story is that you've been given the day off to visit your mother because she's sick. That I.D. is worth something only if you believe in it yourself! But you know all that. Okay, go pack your suitcase."

"Yes, but . . . my uncle has forbidden me to set foot outside the door."

William broke into laughter. "Poor boy," he teased. "Won't your big bad uncle let you go outside to play with the other boys and girls?"

"Honest! I had to promise him."

"What did you have to promise?"

"That I'd have nothing to do with the underground and that I wouldn't set foot outside the door."

"How long have you been here?"

"Ever since the day we left with Van der Mey."

"And you've been locked up here since then? No wonder you're looking so sickly. You've never been outside since then?"

"Not much."

"You're nuts, man!" William exploded. "So, you gave your promise. Do you intend to keep that promise?"

John didn't answer.

"What happens if you don't?"

"Then I mayn't come back."

"So what? Who said anything about coming back? Listen, we need you!"

"What for?"

"A caper."

"A caper?"

"Yes! We're going to rob a distribution centre. We need ration cards. It really isn't very dangerous; it's all been planned out beautifully. Man, I'm telling you, we've got a topnotch group! And our landlady is terrific! She's seventy years old. But we're one man short, so I told our chief about you. He said, 'That's our man! How do we get hold of him?' So here I am. I've come to take you away."

"Where to?"

"You'll see. All I can tell you now is that it's close to Amersfoort."

"But how did you find me, William?"

"No problem," grinned William. "I know this pretty little lady who knows all about you."

"Rita?"

"How did you guess?"

"You mean you've been to Rotterdam?"

"Sure, why not?"

"Weren't you afraid you'd be recognized?"

"Listen, John, it's high time you got out of here. Otherwise, pretty soon you won't dare to come out at all. That's what happens when people go into hiding and have nothing to do but think about themselves. We've got work for you, man! Now move! Go shave yourself. You look like a bum! You need a haircut, too, but we'll take care of that later. Don't you have anything to drink? You're sure a lousy host."

"We've got some imitation tea."

"No, thanks. I'd sooner drink water. Well? Have you decided?"

"Let me think a minute," John said. It was all happening so fast.

He got up and went to the bathroom to shave. He hoped that William would leave him alone for a while. The jubilation in his heart kept being swamped by a cold, muddy wave of fearful thoughts.

16

He lathered his face, looking into the mirror. Two anxious eyes looked back at him. "You know what it means if you go along with William. There's no turning back! Pretty soon you'll be up to your neck in resistance work again — even more deeply than before. You'll be putting everything on the line — your future, Rita, your life. Remember how it felt to run from the Germans? That's how it will be — every day."

"But at least I'd be a free man," he replied to the face in the mirror. "At least I wouldn't have to feel ashamed when I think of the others who are risking their lives. What am I doing here, frittering away my time?"

He jabbed a brush full of lather into the mirror. Then he walked back into the living room, putting a blade into his razor. William lay stretched out on the sofa, his hands behind his head.

"What are you going to do with all those ration cards — if you *do* get hold of them?"

"We'll get them," William assured him. "The ration cards will be distributed all over to help take care of poor divers like yourself who have been forced into hiding. Why?"

"I just wondered. Around here we have to pay 100 guilders for a ration card on the black market."

"Those black marketeers ought to be whipped and flayed!" said William, a steel edge in his voice. "Well, have you made up your mind?"

"I don't know . . ." John got up and went into the bathroom to finish shaving. William followed him and perched on the stool.

"Every member of the group gets double ration cards," he told John. "And we need them. Often that's what we have to pay people to feed us. We're pretty generous to ourselves with our tobacco rations, but that's no skin off anyone else's nose. Sometimes we use them as bribes. We've never *sold* a single ration card.

Did you think maybe we were dealing on the black market?"

"Well, weren't you studying medicine because you wanted to get rich quick?" John teased him. "I wish I could talk to Rita and . . ."

"No need," said William smugly. "I already took care of that. You know what she said? 'Go get him out of there! He's fretting himself to death in that house. I can tell by his letters. John can't take being locked up.' "

"Did she really say that?"

"Would I lie? Well, what do you say?"

He still couldn't make up his mind. That's just the way he was — indecisive. All his life he had been struggling to overcome the inclination to hesitate.

But William knew that once John had made up his mind, you could count on him to stick with it. So he waited patiently and watched as John made tea and set the table like a dutiful housemaid. Then they heard a key turning in the front door. It was John's aunt and uncle, both arriving home at the same time.

Aunt Haddie gave William a warm welcome, but Uncle Herman's face stiffened when he saw him. They both knew him from the time that they had spent two weeks with the De Boers during their last summer vacation. William had been the one in hiding then.

"I thought I'd better drop in on John and see how he was doing," explained William.

"Hmm, yes, of course," said Uncle Herman. And then he began firing questions at William. How did he get their address? What time had he arrived? Did the man across the street see him come in? As William answered Uncle Herman's questions with a smile, John squirmed in embarrassment over his uncle's obvious fear.

"All right," Uncle Herman finally concluded. "I'm sorry, Mr. . . .?"

18

"Just call me William."

"Well, you see, William . . . Let me be honest. I hope you'll understand me right, but I'm not sure you should be seen around here. Don't take this personally, but I'd rather you didn't come again. You see, we've undergone quite enough hardship, with the evacuation and such. I don't want to appear inhospitable, but . . ."

William stood up. "Well, Sir," he said, "since you've already suffered so much hardship. I don't want to cause you any further anxiety. I'd better take my leave."

He walked to the door. Then suddenly John knew what he was going to do. "Wait a minute, I'm coming too," he called to William. "Uncle Herman, I'm sorry, but I have to break my promise to you. You won't have to worry about me anymore, either."

Aunt Haddie and Uncle Herman stared at him, shocked.

"You can't do that!" blurted Uncle Herman. "I promised your father that I'd see to your safety."

"It will be all right with Dad," said John. "Or at least, he'll understand. William needs me."

"William can find somebody else," countered Uncle Herman.

"Sure," said William, "that's what everybody says. Let somebody else pull the chestnuts out of the fire."

John had made up his mind. And although his uncle kept urging him not to go, John could tell that he wasn't really upset about losing his dangerous lodger.

In the end, he was content to let John go after he promised to be careful — as if he were a little boy going out into the street for the first time. He also asked them not to leave before dusk, which was all right with William. They would catch the last train.

John packed his things into a tote bag, and then it was time for supper. The short while after supper was an awkward interlude. Uncle Herman finally began correcting a pile of student papers. This gave William a sudden idea since John was supposed to be a teacher, he should have some papers with him in his briefcase. Uncle Herman rustled up some old examination papers, but only after putting up an argument.

When the time to leave finally came, John wasn't sorry to be saying goodbye, although his uncle gave him a long, emotional handshake. Aunt Haddie's tears were real, and she stood at the door waving until Uncle Herman pulled her inside.

"Where does that Nazi live who worries your uncle so?" asked William.

John pointed across the street.

"Is that his bike?"

"Yes," said John. Taking a deep breath, he felt as if he had shaken off a huge burden. He felt like a new man starting a new life! He felt like running down the block for joy or giving William a good clout on the head with his tote bag . . . But where was William? He had suddenly stopped.

"You go ahead," he said. "I'll catch up with you in a minute."

"What's the matter?"

"I forgot something. Here, you carry my briefcase."

William hurried back down the street and was swallowed up by the gathering darkness. "What could he have forgotten?" wondered John. He sauntered on, feeling exposed. Finally, he stopped and peered down the sidewalk to see if his friend was coming yet. Rrring! It was a bicycle bell right next to him.

"Climb aboard," said William. "We're in a hurry!" Crazy William! Was nothing sacred to him? Grinning, they rode through the darkening city on the beautiful bicycle of the Nazi bureaucrat.

CHAPTER TWO

William bought a ticket for John and paid for shipping the bicycle. John envied William's self-assurance. As he followed across the poorly lit landings, he felt conspicuous and vulnerable. But William strode on as if he didn't have a worry or an enemy in the world.

The train was waiting and ready to go. William selected a second-class coach and held open the door for John. The coach was lit by a light the size of a cigarette lighter; you could hardly see your fellow passengers.

John sat quietly in his corner, but he was filled with a warm feeling of belonging to something again. Wheezing and creaking, the train chugged through the dark countryside.

When they got off, airplanes were droning overhead. William was in a hurry now because he wanted to be back before curfew. He got his own bike out of storage and gave John the bike that they had stolen from his uncle's neighbour. The new bicycle rode beautifully, and the thought of the dapper Nazi scouring Amsterdam to find it didn't mar John's enjoyment in the slightest. They pedalled side by side, speeding along the dark roads.

John had no idea where they were. Now they were cycling silently down the streets of a large rural town. The roof of the church rippled with moonlight. House after house went flashing by. From a black garden came the barking of a dog. Finally William turned up a narrow path between two hedges and dismounted to open a gate. Passing through a garden, they groped their way into a shed, where they parked their bikes.

A dog uttered a low growl, but when William spoke a few quiet words to him, he settled down. John felt the big watchdog sniffing his shoes. Not a glimmer of light showed anywhere in the house; it looked as if everyone had gone to bed. But when William tapped out the "V" signal on the door, John heard a bolt sliding back and they stepped into a dark kitchen and the delicious smell of food. Then suddenly the room was flooded with light, and John stood blinking into the face of a frail old woman, who embraced first William and then him.

"So, here you are, my boy," she said, looking him over. "My, my, you sure look peaked, but we'll change that in a hurry. Yes, just take a whiff of that! I saved you some of my bean casserole. You like green beans, don't you? Good! You don't have to call me Madam. We're just plain working people here."

"We all call her Aunt Nellie. That's the way she likes it. Right, Aunt Nellie?" said William. "Whatever you do, don't call her granny, because then she'll put gravel in your soup."

"Well, do I look like a granny?" she said, swivelling her hips and batting her eyelashes like a flirtatious young girl. She took a swipe at William as he tried to plant a kiss on her cheek. "Get! You always know how to get me started. Come on, take John into the dining room, give him a chair, and clear off a corner of the table so you two can eat."

Two young men sat at a table studying a map, while a third sat opposite them writing. As John approached them he saw another fellow slip out the door.

"I still don't like it!" the writer shouted after him.

"Ah, be quiet!" a voice came back from the hall. "Five minutes."

"What's with him?" asked William.

"Oh, nothing," answered one of the others. "You'll see."

As he was introduced, John studied each one closely. The writer, a tall, strong-looking fellow, seemed eager to be friends and gave him such an enthusiastic handshake that John almost winced with pain. While he talked with John, and William set the table, the other two were whispering to each other. Although they kept pointing to the map, John couldn't help feeling that they were talking about him. One of them was slender and fine-featured, with sharp, flashing eyes. The other was in his late thirties, with a receding hairline and a pale, pinched face. He looked at his watch, stood up, and took John by the arm, saying, "Would you come with me for a minute, please?"

"What's going on?" asked William.

But he got no reply. The man took John out into the hall, opened a door, and motioned him inside.

The door closed behind John, and he found himself standing in a room with a round table in the middle. On it stood a vase full of half-wilted flowers. He looked around, mystified, and had just decided to leave when a curtain moved, and suddenly before him stood a German S.S. officer. The man pointed a revolver at him and barked, "Hands up!"

For a moment the room seemed to spin around John, but it was only for a moment. Thoughts flashed through his mind. Was William a traitor? Impossible! Then he, too, had been tricked. Had the house been taken over while William was gone? But what about the nice old lady in the kitchen? It didn't add up. Was this all a nightmare? The steel-gray revolver, however, was very real and so were the hard eyes of the S.S. officer as he shouted, "Hands up!" for the second time. John's hands went up, but his mind asked sharply, "How am I going to get out of here?"

"What's your business here?" the German demanded, stepping closer. There was a noise at the

door; the man glanced away for a second, and John leaped forward, chopping down on the man's gun hand. Pivoting, he grabbed the German by the lapels and flipped him over his hip. The tall officer went flying over a big easy chair, and as he crashed to the floor, John yanked open the door and dived into the hall. He fell right into a tangle of arms and bodies.

He yelped in fear and grabbed for the nearest arm, but then he was buried under a pile of whooping and laughing young men. They had put one over on him. John went limp with relief, but his nerves were still twanging. Everyone was talking to him at the same time. So this is what all the whispering had been about, and why the one fellow had slipped out of the room when he came in.

24

The phony S.S. officer came limping into the hall clutching his rib cage. John still tensed involuntarily at the sight of the gray uniform. He laughed along with the others, but it was a little forced.

The big fellow with the strong grip laughed at the uniformed man. "You sure deserved that! I thought it was a nasty trick."

"I told you he knew judo," said William. "Didn't you believe me?"

John's victim held out his hand.

"I hope you're not offended," he said. "I just wanted to see how much gumption you had. Well, you made it! Say, if you can teach me how to do that, I'll never step aside for another Kraut. Oooh, I must have been convincing, eh? Oooh, I think I've got a couple of cracked ribs."

No one felt sorry for him except Aunt Nellie, who rubbed a little liniment on his bruised ribs after she had served William and John their supper. John barely had time to eat, the group was so busy plying him with questions. They asked him about the things he had been doing, his family, his schooling, past experiences in the resistance, and other details of his life. At the same time, they all told a little about themselves.

John suddenly realized that he had made a good impression and that he was being accepted as a full-fledged member of the group. It was well past midnight when Aunt Nellie shooed them off to bed. Stretching out on the cot in the corner of the attic, John felt alive and grateful. The security he felt here was different and deeper than the security he had felt at Uncle Herman's.

In the next few days, John got to know the whole group, and it didn't take him long to find out the strengths and weaknesses of each man. These seven men, brought together from all corners of the country by the dislocation of the times, had few secrets from each other. Each of them knew that his life depended on the others. Maybe that was why they talked so much — to become united in mind and will so that nothing and no one could separate them.

Uncle Henry was the leader of the group, a short, muscular man in his forties. His ruddy farmer's face and clear blue eyes exuded a stubborn, irrepressible hope. On the night of John's arrival, he had been out to a meeting with other underground leaders. But when he returned the next morning, he took John away from the breakfast table and talked with him for an hour and a half. It amounted to another test for John, a test much more thorough than the stunt of the previous night. The group leader soon knew everything that he wanted to know about John. The strange thing was that John was hardly aware of having said much. The whole interview had been very casual, and Uncle Henry had talked just as much as John.

John learned that as a boy, Uncle Henry had been fascinated by sea stories. At age fourteen he had run away from home looking for a ship. However, his father had caught him and brought him back home, where he had been forced to apprentice to his father, a blacksmith. Later he had wanted to join the army, but his father had opposed that, too. And when it came time for the draft, he was passed over. So he had resigned himself to his lot and finally had taken over the shop from his aging father.

When the Germans invaded the country, he had immediately become involved in the resistance. The critical day came when he was ordered to give the Germans a list of his employees for assignment to work in Germany. He had refused and had been arrested, but he had managed to escape and had gone into hiding. Now he moved about from place to place with his squad like a captain with his ship.

The fellow who had played the role of the German officer was Leo Keizer. His father owned a butcher shop up north. When he had received a draft notice to report for work in Germany, his parents had decided that he should go. But instead he had sought refuge with a friend who lived in the same town as Uncle Henry. Leo began helping in underground work, and when Uncle Henry went underground, Leo joined him at Aunt Nellie's house.

Joe's full name was Joseph Martin Van de Mortel. He was the strong, friendly one with the powerful handshake. He had been a policeman in a large town in the southern part of the country, in Brabant. One day he had been assigned to accompany two N.S.M. inspectors in a search for Jewish divers at a farmer's house. Discovering a four-year-old child huddled in a clothes closet, he had closed the door and locked it, slipping the key back to the farmer's wife. But then one of the inspectors had insisted on looking into the closet for himself, and when the farmer said that he had lost the key, the man broke it open with an ax. Joe hadn't really planned to do anything. But when the Nazi yanked the wailing little boy out of the closet by one leg and began hitting him, something snapped. Joe stepped in front of the inspector and said, "You're letting that child go!" And when the man refused, Joe shot him. As the other Nazi went running from the house, Joe shot at him but missed. Then he jumped on his bike and raced toward the nearby railway station. He managed to catch a train that was pulling out. It was heading north, so that's where he went.

On the train he was tortured by doubts about what he had done. When the train stopped in a town with a Roman Catholic church near the station, he jumped out and went to the church to confess his sin of murder.

After the priest heard his confession, he asked, "What happened to the other inspector?"

"I missed him," said Joe.

"Too bad," said the priest and granted him absolution.

Joe travelled on with a lighter heart. After drifting from place to place, he ended up at Aunt Nellie's.

Pete Kamphuis, the pale fellow who had led John down the hall that night, was a frightened man. At least, that's what he said himself. "Everything I've done," he often said, "I've done out of sheer terror." He had been head of a distribution office somewhere in the province of Overyssel and had been smuggling ration cards to the resistance movement.

"I didn't really dare to do it," he told them. "But I didn't dare say no to those hard-nosed underground workers, either. Gradually, more and more people were going into hiding, so the underground needed more and more ration cards. I went too far, and I knew that one day the auditors would show up. I was afraid to wait for that day, so I ran. Yes, I took along all the ration cards in the office, but only because I was afraid of what my friends would say if I left them behind."

Sometimes Pete would sit staring into space, not hearing a word of what the others were saying. He had left a wife and a four-year-old daughter behind, and he hadn't seen them for almost six months. "I'm afraid that soon they won't know me anymore," he told John.

Pete stayed close to Robert Brand, who claimed that he didn't know what it meant to be scared. His sensitive face would darken and his eyes flash with hatred when he talked about the ideology of National Socialism.

He had been a student in Delft. When all the Jewish professors were dropped from the faculty, he became a leader in the student strike which finally forced the closing of the university. He subsequently worked for a secret student paper, travelled around the country with a small theatre group, and then began distributing the underground Communist newspaper called *The Truth*. In the process, he became very skilful at forging I.D. cards. He had also helped English fliers get back to England and tossed bombs into German trucks.

Once the S.D. had surrounded a house he was visiting. They were looking for him. He couldn't find a place to hide in the apartment, and he ran into a girl's room. There he put on a dress, borrowed a purse, tied on a kerchief, and walked out through the front door with small, ladylike steps. He passed right between the Germans and strolled away. Since then he had become so attached to his female disguise that he had made an extra I.D. for himself under the name of Evelyn Adams.

Except for the war, these young men would probably never have met each other. But now they were being moulded into one family, with Uncle Henry as the father and Aunt Nellie as the mother.

Aunt Nellie never seemed to be frightened, and she could put on a brilliant performance. Not long after John arrived, she took him into town to buy him some clothes. They walked down the street arm in arm. She had decided to pass him off as the son of her deceased sister. On the way downtown they ran into one of her friends, who stopped to chat for a minute.

"Guess what!" said her aging friend. "Yesterday someone came and asked me if I would hide a diver in my house!"

"Oh, my goodness!" cried Aunt Nellie. "And what did you say? You didn't do it, did you?"

"Why not?" said her friend. "Don't you think it's proper? Almost everybody's got a diver these days. I *did* say to him that he couldn't keep on with that illegal business. 'You've got to be good if you stay here,' I said."

"I should say! You've sure got nerve," Aunt Nellie told her, squeezing John's arm. "But if I were you, I'd keep quiet about it. If I had divers in my house, I'd be on my toes every minute. I sure wouldn't tell anyone about it — not even my closest friends."

The first few days there was nothing to do. The men hung around the house, did a little reading, helped Aunt Nellie once in a while, and bided their time until the distribution-centre hold-up. They were waiting for the signal that the new ration cards had arrived and were tucked away in the safe at the centre. This raid should yield between seven and eight thousand cards, a number that would make it well worth the trouble and risk.

One day when William and Leo were away, Uncle Henry came home with what he called "a nice little job." They could take care of it while they were waiting for the go-ahead on the big caper.

In a town about two hours away by bike, the people were being harassed by a policeman who badly needed to be taught a lesson. The man wasn't an out-and-out traitor; he didn't belong to the N.S.M. But he blindly carried out all the orders issued by the German authorities. A warning in the form of an anonymous letter from the underground hadn't made much of an impact on him. Maybe a more dramatic warning was needed. Suppose someone ambushed him and stripped him of his uniform and weapon?

A great idea! Itching to do something, the men jumped at Uncle Henry's plan. They would teach him his lesson. Besides, they could use another gun. The group's arsenal was woefully inadequate. They had Joe's revolver, an old horse pistol, and a set of brass knuckles.

This would be a good job for Joe and John, Uncle Henry decided. Joe, because he had been a policeman himself, and John, because he could pin the man with a judo hold.

"What about me?" asked Robert, alias Evelyn, in a falsetto voice. "The boys go out and have fun, but the girls stay home, right?" He put on such an indignant pout that Uncle Henry guffawed.

"What did you have in mind?" he asked.

"Well," said Evelyn, "I thought I'd go out with these two handsome boys to help throw a scare into that hard-headed policeman. Nothing like a little feminine charm to make a man forget his duty."

"What about you, Pete?" asked Uncle Henry. "Can you hang around here to take messages — just in case?"

"Oh, I guess," said Pete, slouching down in his chair. The others were suddenly full of life, though John also felt a sudden sinking feeling in his stomach. Joe wanted to leave right away!

"Don't forget the ammo for the pistol," Uncle Henry reminded him. Joe saluted.

"Your word is my command, Sir!"

CHAPTER THREE

The sky looked like rain as they neared their destination, so they stopped to put on their slickers. Evelyn tied on a kerchief and checked his makeup in a mirror.

"Careful," warned Joe, "or we'll have all the boys in town chasing us."

Evelyn gave them a scornful sniff. "Do I have to put up with clods and boors all my life?"

He swung his leg over the bar, rearranged his skirt, and pedalled on again. At a fork in the road, two policemen came hurrying out from beneath a tree and ordered them to stop. A middle-aged man with a corpulent face and a big black mustache demanded to see their I.D.'s. John's pulse raced as he handed over his phony I.D. It was the first time he had been asked to show it since he had become a wanted man. But he controlled himself and kept his hand extended to take back the card. Father had made it, so he was sure it was all right. See, the man was already handing it back. Neither of the other two I.D.'s raised any suspicion either. They could go on.

"Do you ever catch anybody?" Joe asked, trying to be friendly.

The young policeman looked at the older one, who asked, "Why? What business is it of yours?"

"Oh nothing. Just asking."

"Well, you're just asking too much."

"Okay, I'm sorry!" said Joe with a shrug. "I didn't mean to pry. Would you like a smoke?"

The young policeman took one, but the older one shook his head. He did become a little friendlier however.

"On vacation?" he asked.

"Right," said Joe.

"Two whole weeks away from the office!" sighed Evelyn.

"Where are you headed?" the older man wanted to know.

"Now *you're* asking too much," Joe replied. "But just because we don't know ourselves where we're going. We're on a vacation without goals and without schedules; we just go where the spirit takes us."

"He's talking too much," John thought to himself. And Evelyn told him as much as they cycled into town: "The less you say, the better. Your southern accent gives you away. Now those two policemen will have a pretty good picture of us in their minds."

Joe nodded. "I thought maybe the fat one with the mustache might be our man," he said. "He looks like the kind who goes by the book."

They rode down a broad street that led them straight to a beautiful old church. This had to be the right Street. Number 12 Church Street was the address they had been given. They were supposed to see a lawyer who was on the town council. The plan was that one of them would go to the house and ask to borrow a bicycle pump.

Joe and Evelyn rode on while John stopped in front of number 12. He had a moment of doubt however. This house seemed too small and rundown to be the house of a lawyer. But this was number 12 and it was on Church Street. Come to think of it, however, he hadn't seen the name of the Street anywhere. Joe or Evelyn must have seen it, because they had seemed sure enough.

"Good evening, Madam," said John. "Could I please borrow your bicycle pump. I . . . ."

"The bicycle pump? Why, of course," she replied.

The response gave John a scare. That wasn't the answer that they had agreed on. The reply was supposed to be, "Did Uncle Henry send you?" Uncle Henry had arranged the passwords. Had the woman forgotten?

Joe came riding back as John stood outside the door waiting.

"Wrong place," he hissed. "Come on!"

But John hesitated; it wouldn't be smart to take off now. The woman was just coming back with the pump and she handed it to him. It was an old one, and it squeaked with every stroke.

"I guess my husband should oil the thing," she said. "Does it work all right? My, you've sure got a beautiful bike. Where are you from?"

"Yes, it is a nice bike, thank you," John responded, handing back the pump and hurrying to be gone. That was probably a mistake, he thought as he rode off. He should have fed her some story.

Joe was waiting at the church, and Evelyn had gone on to the right house. Church Street was on the *other* side of the square. When they rode up to number 12, Evelyn was already inside, standing at the living room window. He signalled to them to go around the back. There they were met by the lawyer, Mr. Boonstra, a man with straw-coloured hair, a narrow face, and gray eyes.

They told him about stopping at the wrong address, and John suggested that they take another road on the way back. But Boonstra said not to worry. "I know those people," he said. "They're sound, though maybe a bit too free with their tongue. But I'll drop in on them and warn them before you leave. Did you fellows eat yet? Well, then you'd better shake a leg. The table's set!"

John enjoyed being part of a real family once again, sitting around a big table with several children. They didn't seem the least bit awed by the sudden company. These visits must happen more often in this household. The youngest boy, a child of about five, couldn't take his eyes off Evelyn. He watched Evelyn eat with obvious fascination. Maybe it was the lipstick and makeup. Not many women used makeup in rural towns like this one.

"Mommy," he said suddenly, pointing at Evelyn, "that lady has a thing in her neck just like Daddy. A little bump that wiggles when she eats."

Everyone at the table burst into laughter, but the threesome looked at each other in amazement. This little five-year-old was more observant than most adults; his adam's apple was the weakest point in Evelyn's disguise. He should really wear a blouse with a high collar.

After supper, the men withdrew into the lawyer's study to discuss the business that had brought them together. Mr. Boonstra had a plan. The policeman would have to be lured away from home. John and Evelyn should pretend that they had been molested by a drunk, suggested Boonstra. Then they would lead him to a deserted road at the south end of town, only a few blocks from the man's house, where Joe would be staggering around as if he were drunk. When the man tried to collar Joe, the three of them would overpower him and knock him out with chloroform.

Yes, they could get some chloroform from the town doctor, and yes, he was sound. The best time would be around ten o'clock; by that time, since there was no electricity, most people would have gone to bed.

They examined the plan for weaknesses and finally approved it. The lawyer telephoned the local doctor and told him that Bobby was sick. It looked like the measles, he said. The doctor arrived within a few minutes, bringing a bottle of chloroform and some gauze pads.

Once again they rehearsed the plan down to its smallest details. Evelyn objected to the idea of using a drunk as a ruse, for there was little or no liquor available anymore. But the doctor eased his mind on that score. Whenever the local farmers got together, there was plenty of liquor for everybody. With their butter and pork, the farmers could get anything they wanted, and they seemed to be drinking more now than before the war. No, that wouldn't rouse the policeman's suspicions.

Mr. Boonstra had drafted a letter that was to be pinned to the man's chest. After they made a few changes, Evelyn printed out the message neatly on a card. It read:

Your weapons and uniform have been confiscated by order of the government-in-exile because you have shown yourself unworthy of them by serving the interests of the enemy. If you conduct yourself as a loyal citizen from now until the end of the war, the full honours of your office will be restored to you. If you do not, you have forfeited your right to live, and you will be sentenced to death. All your actions are being recorded. Tread carefully!
For the government,
— The Underground

"Can we do that?" John asked doubtfully. "Speak on behalf of the government?"

"Of course!" said Evelyn. "Didn't you hear what Uncle Henry said this morning? From now on we represent the law in this country. As long as the legal government can't enforce the law, it's our duty to do so. That's the way it is! Don't worry your head about that, my boy."

"Boy," he called John, and the doctor's condescending smile said the same thing. The latter had ignored him from the beginning, addressing himself to Joe and Evelyn. Maybe he could sense how John felt — hesitant and fearful. That's how he always felt beforehand, but when it came time to act, that would pass. Unless, of course, he was asked to do something contrary to his conscience. He had to be sure that what he was doing was right. A prayer for strength formed in his heart.

Now they had to plan for their getaway after the job was done. The sooner they were gone, the better! They studied a map provided by Mr. Boonstra and discovered a bicycle trail that passed near the spot of the ambush. Much of it wound through forests and along railroad tracks and it would take them a long way toward home. They wouldn't get home until long after curfew, but that was a risk they would have to take. Mr. Boonstra produced a flashlight powered by a small generator that you operated by squeezing a lever on the handle. Every time you squeezed, the light made an asthmatic, wheezing sound.

"I call it my panting hart," said Mr. Boonstra.

"Panting hart?"

"Sure, 'As the hart pants after the water brooks . . .' You know the text."

They waited for nightfall over a cup of tea. Had it not been for the job that lay ahead, John would have enjoyed the evening with the lawyer's family, but now he was fighting a sense of fear and uncertainty. Was he losing his nerve?

He was immensely relieved when ten o'clock finally came around and Evelyn said that it was time to leave. At the door the doctor shook hands with each of them, giving Evelyn a long, hearty farewell and John only a brief, casual goodbye. But what did he care what the doctor thought? He wasn't in it for recognition, was he?

A light drizzle was falling when they got outside; the weather was being very cooperative. Mr. Boonstra led them to the ambush site and showed them how to get to the bicycle trail from there. Leaving their bikes with Joe near the spot where he was to put on his act, Evelyn and John followed Boonstra to the policeman's house.

"Up ahead! Where the gate's standing open. See it?" whispered Boonstra. "Success!"

He gave them each a quick handshake and retreated into the darkness.

"Let's go!" said Evelyn, pulling him toward the gate. They found their way up the path to the door of the house. Groping along the doorpost, they searched for a doorbell until they saw the old-fashioned knocker in the middle of the door. Evelyn rapped several times, quickly; then he took John's arm and went into his act. He panted as if he had been running hard and trembled as if he had had a terrible fright.

Heavy footsteps sounded in the hall, and a small window in the door was jerked open.

"Yes, who is it?" demanded an unfriendly voice.

"Are you the police, Sir? We were just . . ." And Evelyn went into his story. They were just out for a walk when they were accosted by a strange man, who had gotten very violent, and . . .

"Wait a minute," said the voice. The door opened, and they stepped into a narrow hallway. The door shut behind them, and the hallway light was switched on. They found themselves face to face with a corpulent man wearing the white shirt and blue pants of a policeman's uniform and a big black mustache. The one from the road check! He recognized them immediately.

"Hah, the vacationers! Right?"

"Isn't that a coincidence!" exclaimed John. "Yes, we thought this was such a pretty town that we would stay overnight. And just now as we were out for a walk . . ."

"Where are you staying?" the policeman interrupted.

"In the hotel," said Evelyn. "Nice place, good food. Much better than we can get in the city. But that man gave me such a scare, I'm afraid to walk back. He should be locked up!"

"The Forest View Hotel?" the policeman persisted.

"Is that the name? Yes, I think that's the one," said John. All his fear had left him. Without waiting for cues, he picked up Evelyn's story. The man had been

ugly drunk and wouldn't allow them to pass. He had
followed them and become very lewd and threatening.
They had started running, and he had tripped and
fallen, and they hadn't seen him get back up.

"How did you know where to come for help?" asked
the policeman.

"He's suspicious," thought John, but he answered
in a flash, "We asked someone where we could find a
policeman."

"Yes," said Evelyn, "a woman we passed on the
road."

"He had insulted her, too," added John. "She pointed out your house and said, 'Go there, he's always ready to help.' "

"She said that?" the man said with a pleased look. He went to the coat rack and put on his coat. Beside it hung his billy club and his holster. He grabbed his billy club, but left his gun on the rack.

John and Evelyn looked at each other. It was just a glance, but the policeman caught it.

"What's the matter?" he asked. "Something wrong?"

"Yes," said Evelyn, shuddering, "my fiancé wants me to go along. But that man gave me such a fright, I'd rather stay here, if you don't mind."

"This is no business for women," he growled at John. Motioning to Evelyn, he said, "Follow me," and led him into the kitchen, where his wife and daughter sat shelling peas. Evelyn took a chair that was offered him but clutched his coat around him and began reciting the whole story all over again, trying to sound a bit hysterical. When he heard the front door slam, he heaved a couple of dramatic sighs, rolled his eyes and moaned, "I'm afraid all this excitement has made me sick to my stomach. May I use your bathroom, please?"

The policeman's wife pointed out into the hall. Evelyn slammed the bathroom door, quietly darted down the hallway, and lifted the holster from the coatrack. It was only two steps to the front door. As he turned the knob, he heard a noise behind him. The policeman's wife was standing at the end of the hall, her mouth open and her hands clutching her chest.

"I've just got to see what's happening!" Evelyn said, trying to save the situation as he tried to conceal the stolen weapon under his coat. Before he reached the gate, he heard a piercing scream behind him, which he was sure could be heard for several blocks.

Meanwhile, John had gone off into the night with the policeman. His self-confidence didn't abandon him. He remembered what Uncle Henry had said before they left: "Of course, a job has to have a plan! It should be planned down to the smallest details. But count on it: no matter how well you've figured everything out, something unexpected will happen, and the plan has to be changed. Whatever you do, don't let that throw you! Adjust to the new situation." Well, he and Joe should be able to overpower the man. And then they would have to go back for Evelyn.

The fat policeman was chatting amiably. The town had started construction on a new town hall, but the building couldn't be finished now. He bragged about the beautiful forests in the area. An excellent system of bicycle paths carried you through some of the prettiest scenery in the country, he said. They really ought to cycle out to the lookout tower a few kilometres north of town.

The man didn't seem to be such a bad sort. But in a few minutes he would be stripped and lying unconscious in a ditch. John was starting to feel sorry for his chubby companion.

And the policeman strolled along as if he had all night. Ahead lay the railroad tracks. The place of ambush was only a block beyond. But as they approached the crossing, bells began to ring and lights began to flash. A train was coming! The automatic gates came down, blocking their path.

Suddenly the policeman quickened his pace. Ducking under the gates, they scrambled across the tracks just ahead of a slow freight train. Behind them a motorcycle was just pulling up to the crossing. Then they were both dazzled by a searchlight. John caught the gleam of light on wet helmets. A German motorcycle and sidecar!

"Heil Hitler!" shouted the policeman, extending his arm in the Nazi salute. All John's pity for the man evaporated.

As they walked on, someone came running behind panting heavily. It was Evelyn. He must have just made it under the crossing gates too.

"What's this?" exclaimed the policeman in exasperation. "I thought you were staying behind? Is something wrong?"

"Oh, officer," gasped Evelyn, "I couldn't stand it any longer. I was sure something dreadful would happen to my fiancé. Oh, look! Look! Over there!"

Ahead of them a dark figure lurched out into the road from between some trees. A drunken voice carried through the night: "A ring when it's rolling breaks no bones . . ."

"Hey, you! Come here!" shouted the policeman, slowly approaching Joe.

John got ready to grab him, and Evelyn was shrieking and hanging on the policeman's arm.

"Oh, be careful, be careful!"

As Joe charged, John grabbed for the man's other arm.

The policeman screamed for help, but just then the train thundered by through the crossing. The man was powerful; he wrestled his right arm free and came up with his billy club, swinging wildly. But John twisted his other arm behind his back until the policeman arched backward in pain. This enabled Joe to get the chloroform-soaked gauze over his face. In a few seconds, the big man lay limp in John's arms. They dragged him onto the shoulder of the road. Evelyn was ripping at the man's buttons, and Joe ran to get the tote bag. The tail end of the train passed through the crossing.

"The revolver!"

"I've got it already."

"What about the billy club?"

"Leave it, it's probably out on the road somewhere. Hurry!"

"Give me the note."

Loud voices sounded from town. A motorcycle engine was revved up.

"Go! Go! They're coming!"

John didn't take the time to pin the note on the man's shirt but quickly tucked it under his undershirt. Fear came rushing back. His bike, where was it? Joe was already racing off. There was Evelyn. He had John's bike, too. "At your service," he said.

On the bike. Pedalling for all he was worth. After Joe. A loud crash sounded behind him, as if someone had fallen to the road. Where was Evelyn? He put on his brakes and looked back. Then Evelyn went shooting past. "Come on, faster!" he shouted. Down the road came a single headlight. Another light, a searchlight, scanned the woods on both sides of the road. The German soldiers! One after the other, the three bicycles skidded around the corner onto the bicycle trail. Not ten seconds later, the motorcycle went roaring past. The Germans had missed them.

Then they heard the squeal of tires and loud voices. The soldiers must have realized their mistake and were coming back. Soon the searchlight was playing down the forest trail, but they were already out of reach. Zzzing! A bullet whizzed overhead, and several others went rattling through the pine trees on either side of the trail. They bent down over their handlebars and sped on. The motorcycle couldn't follow, because with a sidecar it was too wide for the narrow forest trail. But what if they disconnected the sidecar? How long would that take?

"Look out! On the right!" shouted Joe. Two trails crossed here, and they had to make a right-hand turn. They took the corner without slowing down. Then Evelyn was suddenly dropping behind and making strange noises. John stopped. Evelyn couldn't pedal anymore because he was laughing so hard.

"Listen," he said, "you know what happened to me back there? When I jumped on my bike, I forgot all about my skirt and fell flat on my face. But look what I found as I was rolling around on the road — the billy club! Here, Joe, put it in the bag. Take the holster too. Phew! You smell like a walking laboratory."

"Keeps the mosquitos away," Joe said.

They examined their most important prize, the police revolver, by the light of Boonstra's "panting hart." It was well cared for. Joe opened the cylinder.

"It's loaded," he said, satisfied. "It shouldn't be too hard to get more ammo for this thing. How about a quick rest, fellows? We're okay here. If we hear anyone coming, we'll duck into the trees."

The brief rest helped them to relax a little. They kept their eyes and ears wide open, but the only sound was the rustling of the wind in the treetops. The rain had stopped, and the narrow ribbon of the paved bicycle path glistened in the moonlight. John felt his leg beginning to throb where he had taken a mean kick from the fat policeman. Joe studied the map by the light of the wheezing flashlight.

"Okay, boys, I've got it now," he said. "Let's go! No more talking, and keep your eyes open when we get to the highway. We'll have to be especially careful when we get close to town. They may have put out an alarm to the surrounding towns."

The threesome pedalled on at a steady pace. John could see the backs of his companions ahead of him. Occasionally, a quiet warning or a muted cough reached his ears. Every now and then, he got a whiff of chloroform. As he looked at their bent backs, a strong affection for his two companions welled up inside him.

They arrived home just a little after midnight. They marched up to the table in front of Uncle Henry one at a time and each ceremoniously deposited a piece of the booty on the table — the revolver, the billy club, and the hat and badge. Uncle Henry played his part, receiving each article with a bow and making a little speech in honour of the occasion. Then he gave them each a place of honour: Joe on his left, Evelyn-Robert on his right, and John beside Aunt Nellie.

The whole group had been waiting up. A pot of coffee was perking on the stove, and Aunt Nellie had baked a cake. The room was filled with the happy awareness that they were all safely back together again.

Joe told what had happened, with John and Evelyn filling in. From his pocket Joe pulled the empty chloroform bottle and the gauze. The smell immediately filled the room, and Joe dashed for the garbage can. Uncle Henry complimented him for not leaving them at the scene of the ambush:

"Don't ever leave a single trace behind you, if you can help it." He seemed quite satisfied with the way that they had carried off the job. But he was a little worried about Mr. Boonstra.

"More people must get those two streets confused," he said, "and if those first folks don't keep their mouths shut, Boonstra could be in trouble! He'd better see to it that his house is clean."

"You were extremely fortunate to get away from those German soldiers," said Uncle Henry. "We ought to get down on our knees and thank God for the way everything worked out."

Even Evelyn-Robert, who professed to be an agnostic, nodded.

"Is that the whole story?" asked Uncle Henry. "What are you grimacing about, John?"

"That big policeman gave me a little souvenir," said John, pulling up his pantleg. His knee was swollen, and a purple bruise was spreading up onto his thigh.

"Hmm, the man certainly knows how to kick," observed Uncle Henry. But Aunt Nellie clucked her tongue and hurried off to get some cold compresses.

Meanwhile, Uncle Henry told them that he also had some good news. He had come across a couple of places that should be easy to crack — a town hall and another distribution centre. The latter he would investigate further tomorrow, and then they would discuss it again. Nobody was going to get bored, he promised them.

"Anybody else have anything important to report?" asked Uncle Henry, using the billy club as a gavel. "Otherwise I'll adjourn this meeting."

Pete raised his hand.

"I don't know if you think this is important," he drawled, "but I was listening to the news tonight, and the announcer said that the Allies had finally set foot on European soil. Today they landed on Sicily."

"Not important! How blasé can you get!"

"You knew that all evening, and you didn't say anything? Man, have you got sawdust in your veins?"

"What's so great about Sicily?" Pete demanded. "It's not exactly next door, you know."

"No, but it's the beginning, it's the beginning!"

Once again, they felt that they weren't fighting alone. The Germans were being attacked from within and without, and the Allies wouldn't stop hammering until the Nazis were gone. It might not be long now! Uncle Henry stood up and began to sing the national anthem.

Quietly, so that the neighbours wouldn't hear, they all joined him. The clock, too, chimed in, striking twice.

CHAPTER FOUR

The next morning, just after Joe and William had left to contact a resistance worker in another town, the long-awaited call about the distribution centre raid arrived: "Grandpa is celebrating his eightieth birthday tonight. Family members are asked to be there no later than six o'clock."

Uncle Henry swore quietly as he put down the phone. It was too late to catch Joe and William. They'd have to do the job with five men. And Uncle Henry had recruited John because he had figured that six wouldn't be enough. The "eightieth birthday" meant a bigger haul than they had expected. And the original plan had been for eight o'clock. Uncle Henry called a meeting to review and revise the original plan.

"What shall we do, boys?" he asked.

"Let's go!" three of them replied. "We can see what happens when we get there."

"What do you say, Pete?"

Pete was writing a letter to his wife. He chewed on the end of his pen.

"Yes, what should I say? It wouldn't be polite to keep all those people waiting . . ."

"So, that's settled," said Uncle Henry. "We go! And if we all work twice as hard as usual, we've got three more men than we need."

John looked at their leader; his clear eyes calmed the fear that was rising in his throat. When he was around, you felt like nothing terrible could happen.

Once more they reviewed the original plan down to its smallest details. They studied the floor plan of the distribution centre and the map of the area. Then, after having a sandwich and coffee, they lay down for a while to rest. No one even tried to sleep.

At three-thirty they were ready to leave. This time Evelyn-Robert was dressed in a neat gray skirt and a high-collared blouse; in his large purse he carried on-ion sacks, belts, lengths of cord, and several bandannas. Ration cards would go in the sacks, to be strapped with the belts on the back of their bikes. They might have to use cords and bandannas to tie and gag the guards. Evelyn would also carry the guns concealed under his skirt. They were relatively safe there, for the police rarely frisked women during checks.

Had they forgotten anything? "Yes," said Uncle Henry, "the most important thing of all. Come here and sit down, boys. First we'll ask God's blessing on our work. We're fighting for justice and righteousness, and we don't have to do that in our own strength."

Everyone was silent. Evelyn, too, sat reverently with his head bowed. Uncle Henry said quietly, "Lord, Thou knowest everything. Thou knowest what we're about to do. Thou hast laid this work on us, and we put ourselves in Thy keeping. Save us from our enemies, but also save us from doing what is evil in Thine eyes. Lead us and give us strength."

Then John knew the mysterious force which radiated from Uncle Henry: it was his great trust in God. Now they all seemed to share it. They said goodbye to Aunt Nellie as if they were going out on a bicycle trip. Pete began to make some wisecrack as he shook her hand, but then she pulled him toward her and kissed him on both cheeks. And she did the same to all her boys.

"Try to be back before eleven," she said. "I'll have a special supper waiting. None of you ate very much this noon, and you'll all be hungry."

Their destination was forty kilometres away. They planned to cycle the return distance in two hours; now they had to save their energy. They pedalled to the nearest town, and each of them bought his own ticket and a baggage card for his bike. Then they hung around on the station platform waiting for the local train to show up.

It was a busy station. The town was full of retired couples and vacationers. Uncle Henry and Pete were together; John was walking arm in arm with Evelyn; and Leo stood by himself. They pretended not to know each other.

They travelled in different coaches and got out at different stops. One group detrained one stop early; another, one stop late. But at six o'clock they had met at the prosperous-looking home of Mr. Muller, an official at the distribution centre. Although the man was of German ancestry, he was risking his life to help the underground. A short, chubby man with thick, round glasses, he was much sharper than he looked.

The ration cards had arrived the night before under police escort, Mr. Muller told them. Distribution of the cards would start early the next morning, so the job couldn't be delayed. The usual procedure was for the person who locked up in the evening to bring the safe key to the police station, where the chief would pick it up the next morning. Except for one man, the police were all sound men who cooperated with the underground. The original plan had called for one of the policemen simply to borrow the safe key and then put it back after the burglary.

"But we've recently gotten a new mayor, thanks to Mr. Mussert, the head of the National Socialist Movement," explained Mr. Muller. "And he must have become aware of the policemen's sympathies, because today, after the cards came, he suddenly ordered us to bring the key to his place instead of the police station. So tonight the key is hanging in the mayor's house."

"And you don't think he'd be willing to lend it to us for a little while, eh?" Uncle Henry asked drily.

"I don't think so. At least, not willingly," said Mr. Muller, smiling. "I've been trying to think of some way to get hold of that key — without success. That is, until now. Seeing the lady in your group gives me an idea how you can get into his house."

"What would you do without us women?" said Evelyn, with a sigh of satisfaction.

"Last week the mayor's wife put an ad in the local paper for a housekeeper," Mr. Muller explained. "I'm quite sure that no one has responded, for there are very few girls in this town willing to work for someone who belongs to the N.S.M. Now, if this young lady were to apply for the position . . ."

"Out of the question," said Evelyn with a sniff. "I've never been anything less than a governess, and I'll not demean myself."

But of course Evelyn went along with the plan. Again John was to accompany him as his fiancé. They made a convincing couple.

"How big a family is it?" asked John.

"The mayor, his wife, and two daughters," said Muller. "The mayor's younger brother has been staying with them, too. He's with the S.S. and is due to leave for Russia any day. He was still there yesterday, and no one has seen him leave — at least, not by train. No one has seen him around today either, so he may have been picked up by car. We're not sure one way or the other."

"What about the guards at the distribution centre?" asked Uncle Henry.

"There are two of them," said Muller. "One of them is okay, but the other is the one bad apple I mentioned. He's a rabid National Socialist, so be very careful with him. He'll shoot you to pieces and think he's being a hero."

"Well, we can shoot back," said Uncle Henry. "But that would spoil the caper. Then we'd have to speed out of there without the cards. We'll have to get the jump on him! That will be your job, John."

"The other guard has asked that you don't treat him too gently," Muller went on, "because the N.S.M. man mustn't suspect anything. They think he's been put on the force as a spy, so the others have to watch out for him."

"Okay, we'll see to it that he gets his share of the lumps. What time do we hit the place? Eight-thirty, as we agreed?"

"Yes," said Muller, "it should be starting to get dark by then. The watch changes at eight o'clock. If you do a smooth job, chances are it won't be discovered until tomorrow morning. Don't forget, we need some ration cards here ourselves. About 600 should do. One of our local men will be behind the building to take them off your hands. The password will be 'Sicily.' We're not being too greedy, are we?"

"Greedy?" repeated Uncle Henry, laughing. "Even if you asked for half of them, we'd still be happy."

Mr. Muller leaned forward in his chair and cleared his throat. "I want to tell you men how much I admire your courage and your willingness to put your lives on the line for all of us. I'm afraid I could never . . ."

"Horse-feathers!" exclaimed Uncle Henry. "You've practically wrapped, sealed, and delivered this deal single-handedly. Without men like you, we would be exactly nowhere!"

Mr. Muller looked at him with a sceptical but appreciative grin, and then took off his glasses and began polishing them.

At a quarter past eight, John and Evelyn were walking up the front steps of the mayor's mansion. John felt no fear at all. His revolver felt bulky in his right coat pocket. He kept fighting the impulse to touch it. Evelyn also had a gun in his pocket, but it was the big horse pistol, and he had to keep a kerchief over it to conceal the protruding handle.

A girl of about eighteen opened the door. "How do you do, Miss," Evelyn said. "I'm here about the ad in the paper asking for a housekeeper. Is the job still open? This is my boyfriend."

"Just a minute," said the girl, and she turned back down the hall. As soon as she disappeared, Evelyn and John tiptoed in after her, leaving the front door slightly ajar. They burst into the living room right behind the first daughter. The mayor lay stretched out on the sofa reading a newspaper, his wife was just pouring tea, and the second daughter was curled up in an easy chair with a book.

"Pardon me," said Evelyn, "I thought I'd deliver the message myself. Hands up, everybody!"

"May I introduce you to our leader," said Evelyn with a sweep of his hand. "He'll answer all your questions, and perhaps ask a few of his own."

Then Uncle Henry came walking into the room carrying Joe's revolver. Leo and Pete were already searching the house, and Evelyn joined them. John kept his gun pointed at the mayor.

"The key to the distribution centre safe," barked Uncle Henry. "We want it, and we want it right now! If you cooperate, you have nothing to fear. But if you play games, whatever happens is on your head. Well, what do you say? Speak up!"

"It's not here! It's kept at the police station."

But the wife whimpered in fear. "Tell him the truth. They'll kill us all," she pleaded.

"Please tell him, Daddy," begged one of the girls.

"So, you've lied to us once," said Uncle Henry. "That's the last one you get. For the last time: where's the key?"

"Never mind," came Pete's calm voice from the doorway. "I've already got it. It was lying on his desk in the study. See, it's got a tag on it: Distribution Centre Safe. Wasn't that nice of him?"

He handed the key to Uncle Henry and disappeared.

"Tut-tut, Mr. Mayor, you really should have taken much better care of this key. Are you ever going to get a tongue-lashing when the Germans hear about this! Yes, that's all right Mrs., just put your hands on your neck. It's not as tiring."

Loud laughter sounded in the hall. Into the room came Evelyn and Leo. Between them walked a scowling man in pink pyjamas. "Here's our man for the Eastern front," remarked Evelyn. "But our heroic captain got his footsies wet in the last rain, and now he's got a cold! Dear me, what's going to happen to you in Russia when the temperature drops to 30 below? Yes, that's right, against the wall. My, my, they've taught you well. No need to tremble, Captain, we're not like those nasty Russians. They wouldn't have bothered to wake you up. Just shot you in bed! And thanks for the fine weapon, Sir."

He showed Uncle Henry a heavy nine-millimetre pistol.

"It was next to his bed," said Evelyn. "But I'm afraid he fell asleep at his post, so it didn't do him much good. I think he's forfeited his right to it."

"Nice job," said Uncle Henry. "Well done! But now we've got to find a place to put all these people. Anyone got any ideas?"

Again it was Pete who provided the answer: "I found a beautiful bomb shelter with a boarded-up window and a steel door in the basement. That should keep them safe!"

Rrring! The doorbell! Someone was at the door. Who could that be? Germans? Maybe they had seen something from outside, or maybe someone had tipped them off.

But Uncle Henry was cool. "Evelyn, you go to the door. Give your revolver to Pete. Beside the closet, Pete. Hurry! Leo, take the door across the hall. Keep an eye on them, John."

Uncle Henry followed Evelyn out into the hall. John took a firmer grip on his revolver.

"Just keep those hands high," he snarled at the captain. "I know what you've got in mind. One peep out of you, and I'll blow all the buttons off your pyjamas."

He heard the door being opened.

"Good evening," said Evelyn. "Come in, please. I'm the new maid. Who should I say is calling?"

"Williams," said a deep voice. "So, you're the maid, are you? Well, we're friends of the mayor."

Then came Evelyn's voice again. "Oh, in that case, go right on in. Since you're friends."

Out of the corner of his eye, John saw a man and a woman entering the room, with Evelyn and the others right behind. The woman screamed at the sight of the armed men and of the mayor's family lined up against the wall.

But Evelyn soothed her. "No need to scream, Madam. It isn't as bad as it looks. Would you please join your friends? That's right! Birds of a feather flock together. And you may even join them in the same cage."

Five minutes later, the whole party lay side by side on the basement floor, bound hand and foot and gagged with Aunt Nellie's bandannas. Uncle Henry told Leo to fetch some blankets from the bedrooms for the ladies; the men could do without. "Our captain had better get used to the cold a little if he's going to the Eastern front."

Evelyn was appointed to stay behind to watch the prisoners. He took the teapot and made himself comfortable on the top of the basement stairs. Beside the teapot he put the captain's big pistol.

"Go on," he said, "I'll be okay here. But not so okay that I want to be left behind, so don't forget to pick me up."

John was the last one to leave the house. As he was going out the door, he could hear Evelyn giving the lady of the house a lecture about hoarding. The basement was stocked with all kinds of supplies.

It was a quarter to nine by John's watch when he, Leo, Pete, and Uncle Henry quietly walked their bikes up the alley to the back of the distribution centre and carefully parked them against the wall. The last glimmers of daylight still lingered in the sky.

The old, gray building was completely still. They sneaked along the back, keeping close to the building. There was the bathroom window. It was standing partly open. Some helpful soul had sawed the window bolts halfway through. Uncle Henry easily twisted the window free and lifted it outside.

John took off his coat and shoes. Then four hands lifted him in through the window. His arm scraped the sides of the opening, and then his toes touched something — a radiator. Someone handed him his gun, and he was inside.

Silence. Darkness. Once again fear clutched at his throat. Then, in his mind, he heard the calm voice of Uncle Henry: "Thou hast laid this work on us, and we put ourselves in Thy keeping." He was in good hands.

Quietly, carefully, he eased open the bathroom door. He visualized the floor plan: about thirty feet straight down the hall, through a door, and then to the left. That should bring him to the outside door. The hallway was completely black. He couldn't see a thing. The floor was cold under his stocking feet. One of his socks had a hole in the heel. This must be the corner. Ahead of him, a narrow beam of light cut across the hallway. The guards must be sitting behind that door. He tiptoed by very carefully, his revolver at ready.

"Come on, hurry up!" a voice said. "It's your move."

John touched the front door. The two sliding bolts, well oiled, slid back easily. Then the lock. The key had been left in it; it grated as he slowly turned it. The sound travelled through his bones, and he gritted his teeth. As he took hold of the doorknob, the door was already being opened from the outside.

Uncle Henry was the first to slip inside. He gave John's arm a quick squeeze. John almost laughed out loud at how smoothly things were going. Together they sneaked back down the hall toward the beam of light. There they stopped. Leo and Pete were right behind them.

John peeked inside. Two policemen were sitting at a table playing checkers. One of them was a Nazi collaborator. But which one? It must be the one with the cap. The other one was a jolly-looking fellow, and he had just glanced toward the door. He must know that they were here.

Uncle Henry kicked open the door and everyone rushed into the room.

"Hands up!" he shouted. "Get him, John!"

John grabbed for the policeman's arm as Leo brought down the billy club on his head. The man crumpled to the floor without making a sound.

"Nice going," said the other officer. "Maybe that will knock some sense into his head. I hope that gives him as big a headache as he's been to us."

He shook Uncle Henry's hand and surrendered his revolver. Uncle Henry grabbed him by the uniform and tugged. Buttons clattered to the floor, and a seam gave way with a rip.

"There!" said Uncle Henry. "Now you look like you've been in a fight. How about a shiner? No? You think this will be enough? Okay, boys, let's hustle."

Pete took out the sacks, and John quickly slipped into his shoes and coat. Uncle Henry took the safe key out of his pocket, and they all held their breath as he inserted it, turned the lock, and pulled. The heavy door made a sucking sound as it slowly swung open. There lay the ration cards, neatly sorted into packages of fifty according to kind. For the fifth and sixth period, for milk, butter and meat, for clothes, shoes, gasoline . . .

"Don't just stand there gawking! Come on, stuff them into the sacks. Put six hundred from each period into this sack and keep it separate. Here, give them a little extra. And a few of these specials. Okay, John, take it away!"

John dragged the sack down the dark hallway until he found the back door. Quietly he opened the door and stuck his head outside. He knew what to expect, but he still jumped and banged his head on the doorpost when someone whispered "Sicily" right into his ear. Someone took the sack out of his hands. In the darkness, John couldn't make out his features.

"Everything going all right?" the voice asked softly.

"Perfect," said John. "Hit the road!"

And the man moved off into the darkness, a voice which would remain forever anonymous, one of their many comrades in the underground army of the resistance.

When he got back to the others, the cards were all packed. The last sacks were just being tied shut. The N.S.M. man had revived and sat on the floor rubbing his head and looking groggily around the room. Uncle Henry was at the telephone dialling a number.

"Hello, is this Ludwig? . . . Yes, we're all set. You can bring in the car . . . What? By the school? Okay, we'll see that it gets there . . . No, that's all right. See you later."

Then he took the phone in both hands and yanked the cord out of the wall. Pete and Leo each grabbed one shoulder of the N.S.M. man and dragged him into the safe. Uncle Henry then jammed his pistol into the

other man's ribs and gave him such a shove that he went stumbling forward into the safe and rammed into the N.S.M. fellow. "That's for trying to jump me, you so-and-so! Consider yourself fortunate. I should have shot you!"

They slammed the safe door shut, and quickly carried the sacks out to the bikes and strapped them onto the carriers.

Uncle Henry went ahead to scout and pick up Evelyn. The others followed at intervals of a few hundred feet, their lights masked as prescribed by black-out regulations. Once in a while they met someone, but no one paid any attention to them. They convened in front of the mayor's house.

"So, you bunch of dirty thieves," Evelyn greeted them, "it's about time you showed up!"

They made it home just before the eleven o'clock curfew, having cycled the 40 kilometres in less than two hours. Aunt Nellie's eyes sparkled with thankfulness. They had all returned safe and sound. They had stung the enemy and gotten away scot-free!

After supper they enjoyed the best part of the whole caper — rehashing everything that had happened. It all looked so different now that the suspense and fear were gone. Once again they marvelled at the elderly clerk, Mr. Muller, who had prepared the job with the same precision and attention to detail that he had given all his life to his books. He had even cut through the bathroom window bolts himself. They had a good laugh at the blank expression on the mayor's face when he had suddenly looked up from his newspaper into a gun barrel. And then the doorbell had rung!

"I can't believe it myself," said Pete. "I was as cool as a skate-blade! I stood there by the closet, thinking only that I'd take out as many Germans as I could. I was even a little disappointed when they turned out *not* to be Germans."

"Never mind," said Uncle Henry. "You'll get a chance to do some shooting soon enough if we get any more of these jobs."

"Stop it!" said Aunt Nellie. "If you start talking like that, I'm going to bed."

"Right," said Evelyn-Robert. "You're giving me the chills, talking like that." But at the same time he sat bent over the nine-millimetre pistol, polishing it affectionately.

"Let's have a look at what we risked our necks for," said Leo. "Come on, let's empty these sacks on the table! I'd like to see those pretty colours all mixed together."

But they decided to do it in the attic so that they could wait until morning to sort them. "What's this?" asked Robert, pulling a big brown envelope out of the pile. Printed on the outside in big letters were the words. "Personnel Wages." Inside was 150 guilders and some loose change: according to a balance sheet in the envelope, what was left of the payroll money after the staff had been paid.

"What are we going to do with *that*?" asked Evelyn.

"Yes," said Uncle Henry, "we really weren't supposed to take it. It belongs to the town. I'm starting to feel like a *real* thief."

"Take it back," suggested Pete.

But the robbery would be discovered by morning. Finally they decided to send it back by mail to the Nazi mayor. They would have to mail it from another town, of course. One of them would have to ride to Amersfoort, or Hilversum. While they were getting undressed, the boys thought up a fitting return address: V. Orange, Freedom Road, Queenstown.

"Lenin Road," Evelyn-Robert amended.

"Fine. A little red in the orange won't hurt. They'll call us the Red Royalists. As long as they know what we're fighting for."

"I know! Let's put a note inside: 'Not for riches, but for justice.' "

"Or how about: 'Not for money and might, but for justice and right.' "

They finally agreed on a slogan. They put their weapons on their nightstands or under their pillows, and within a few minutes they were all sleeping the sleep of those who know that they've fought a good fight.

CHAPTER FIVE

During the next few days, most of the ration cards were moved out of the house and put into other hands. Six hundred of the cards were smuggled out to another city by a woman who arrived as a slender girl and left looking like a rather pregnant young woman. A baker from a neighbouring town stopped by to deliver bread and carted off several hundred cards under his baked goods. A post office truck drove up to the house in broad daylight and left with a couple of thousand cards for the city of Amersfoort. The postman filled up two mailbags and tossed them among the others. Small packets of between 20 and 50 were dropped off at several addresses.

Robert, again dressed as Evelyn, took a suitcase full of cards to Leiden, where he had friends in the underground. But he returned the same day with his suitcase still full; his friends already had plenty of cards and couldn't use any more.

"Listen, Uncle Henry!" he said. "There's something wrong with our set-up. We've still got over 3000 ration cards for this period, and we're not going to be able to get rid of them in time. They expire this week. So we stole all those cards for nothing!"

He was right. They were going to be left holding hundreds of expired ration cards, while thousands of divers all over the country were going hungry because they didn't have cards for food. They had to find more contacts.

The only solution was to contact the national organization that collected money for divers — the L.O., which already had a nationwide distribution system set up. Until now, Uncle Henry had been against such a move. He was independent, and he didn't want to take orders from some bureaucrat in a distant city.

Moreover, if a number of people in Amsterdam or The Hague knew of their existence, this would only increase their chances of being betrayed. A single traitor could get them caught. But now he had to admit that they needed such a contact. He went out the same evening to look up a man in the vicinity who had a connection to the L.O. The man promised to pass on Uncle Henry's offer as quickly as possible.

Once the decision had been made, Uncle Henry was content. He had stopped planning further jobs — why risk their lives if they didn't know what to do with the goods? But now he was busy making plans again, and he left early the next morning to discuss the robbery of another distribution centre. Joe went with him.

When they returned that evening, it was obvious that something had gone wrong. Uncle Henry threw down his hat in disgust. The distribution centre in the Achterhoek region had been raided the night before by another underground group. They had netted about ten thousand ration cards. But as they were making their getaway, they had gotten into a shootout with a German patrol. A German officer had been killed, and now the whole town was in a turmoil. The S.D. was turning houses inside out and was even stopping and searching everyone on the streets.

Nevertheless, while Joe waited outside of town, Uncle Henry had managed to get through to his contact man. The man didn't even dare to let him into the house, but Uncle Henry had demanded to know what was going on. The man swore that the other attempt had come as a complete surprise to him. So two groups had been planning the same job at the same time, and Uncle Henry's careful planning and preparation had been in vain. This dramatically revealed the need for cooperation between the scattered little resistance groups.

"What else do we have on the agenda?" asked Robert-Evelyn, who was loafing on the davenport.

"Not much — not for now, anyway," said Uncle Henry, scowling. "Why?"

"Well, I thought if there was nothing cooking for the next few days, I'd like to go to Leiden and have a new I.D. made up for me. I need one. Just take a look at this!"

He reached under his sweater and pulled out the latest issue of the police bulletin, which a co-worker had dropped off that afternoon. Among dozens of other stories was a detailed report of their hold-up of the distribution centre and a shorter one of their ambush of the policeman. Evelyn was described in detail in both reports. The one on the distribution centre caper even gave his name. So one of the group must have spoken it during the robbery.

"Woman dressed in gray suit, above average height, about 25 years old, slender, alto voice, possibly female impersonator. Wow! That mayor and his family must have taken a good look at you, Evie boy."

They tried to tug the magazine out of each other's hands until finally Uncle Henry seized it.

"Attempted murder of policeman," he read.

"I protest!" shouted Joe. "If we had wanted to kill that fat policeman, he would have been dead as a mackerel. It would have been easier if we *had* bumped him off!"

"Be quiet, Joe! Okay, Uncle, read on."

The descriptions of the threesome were surprisingly accurate: Joe and his southern accent, John and his blond hair and ruddy complexion — the main features were all there. The police suspected that the same persons had participated in both crimes, said the bulletin.

"The stolen ration cards were carried off in an automobile," read Uncle Henry, "apparently a Chevrolet sedan."

"Ha, ha! Great!" they shouted, pounding Uncle Henry on the back. "Your trick worked! They've got you riding in style. I wonder where they came up with that make?"

"The apprehension and arrest of the persons described above must be given highest priority. The mayor has offered a reward of 1000 guilders for information leading to the arrest of the perpetrators of said crime." Joe and Leo hooted with laughter. "That chicken-hearted mayor! He must be trying to buy his way back into the good graces of his German superiors. One thousand guilders! Why, that wasn't even 200 guilders apiece. Being a Judas wasn't very profitable these days."

"That's supply and demand," said Robert-Evelyn. "A big supply brings down the prices."

"Well, I'm insulted!" cried Leo. "Next time we're in the neighbourhood, we'll have to show the little bureaucrat that we're worth a whole lot more."

"You've got to agree, though, that Evelyn's days are numbered," said Robert-Evelyn. "I need a new I.D."

"You can get one of those around here," said Uncle Henry.

"Yes, but I'm not easily satisfied," answered Robert-Evelyn. "Half the country is trotting around with false I.D.'s, and most of them are C.C.S. inspectors or assistant pastors. I want a little more status than that. I know someone in Leiden who can get hold of official S.D. papers. I'll be with the German police. With those in my pocket, if a German policeman approaches me on the train, I'll slap him on the back and say, 'Heil Hitler, friend!' I'll be able to carry anything — even weapons.

"You men will benefit too whenever you go out with me. What's safer than travelling with a German police officer? Three days from now, Evelyn will be no more, but from her ashes will rise the most dashing S.D. officer in the country."

"Say, if he's going to take off for a few days, I'd like to go somewhere too," said Leo. "Why sit around here getting bored? I've got some friends just north of here."

"And I . . ." began John.

"Not you, too!" said Uncle Henry. "Where do you propose to go?"

John felt himself beginning to blush as the others looked at him. Did they know that he had a girl in Rotterdam? He hadn't seen Rita for over six weeks now.

"A young man, with blond hair and a ruddy complexion," William quoted from the police bulletin, grinning from ear to ear.

"Well now, seeing as you're all going somewhere anyway," Pete said slowly, as if deep in thought, "then I might as well . . ."

"You want to go see your wife," Uncle Henry finished for him. "But that would be the worst place in the world for you to go. Everybody around there knows you. One word from a traitor or even a gossip, and instead of being in the underground, you'll just be *under* the ground. Of course, you're a free man. You can go where you please. But please stay away from your hometown. Okay?"

"That's all right; I'd probably be too scared to go anywhere near it anyway," Pete drawled, as if talking to himself.

"And well you should be! Listen, boys, I propose that we all take a week's vacation. That will give everybody time to take care of some personal affairs. But in one week I want everybody back here. You got that? One week! That's Wednesday night at ten o'clock. By that time I'll have met with the L.O., and we should have something new on the burner. But keep your eyes and ears open for leads to other jobs! And always keep in mind that it's our job to sabotage the Nazi machine whenever we get the chance."

"No matter what part of the country?" someone asked.

"Of course!" said Uncle Henry. "We're a mobile unit. We serve the whole nation. Another thing. If any of you know where we can get a girl who can smuggle messages and things across the country for us, bring her along. We're going to need her, now that Evelyn is going to commit suicide."

"Ah, she'll be sorely missed," said William, putting on a sad face. "She was Robert's better half."

"And don't bring home a female impersonator by mistake," warned Leo.

"That's right. We want a genuine pretty face around here for a change," said Joe.

They were in a noisy, boisterous mood, but Aunt Nellie was quiet. "And I just got a beautiful piece of beef today," she said sadly. "What am I going to do with it, now that you're all leaving?"

"What! Don't you worry your head about that, Aunt Nellie," they said. "Hey boys, we can't leave Auntie with a big chunk of meat on her hands, or else she'll be fat and lazy when we get back. Who's for a little bedtime snack? Come on, Joe! You know how to fix a steak. Heat up a frying pan. Put some butter in it! We've got plenty of butter cards upstairs. How about it. Aunt Nellie, where are you hiding that steak?"

Aunt Nellie went scurrying about, and they settled down to beefsteak sandwiches after eleven o'clock. Laughing again, Aunt Nellie promised them a similar feast in exactly a week, if they all got home in time. She got a hug and a good-night kiss from all her boys before she went to bed.

The next morning they all left, one after the other. When John stood ready to go, waiting for William, who was going with him part of the way, their local contact man came pedalling to the house with an urgent message for Uncle Henry.

"You're to be in the Café Monopole in Amsterdam at three o'clock this afternoon to meet with the leaders of the L.O.," said the man.

"That was a quick answer," Uncle Henry said, surprised. "How did they respond so fast?"

"No problem," laughed the messenger. "They've been looking for you for several days. They began asking around as soon as they heard about your hold-up of the distribution centre.

"Okay, now listen good! Three o'clock at the Café Monopole. Wait for a well-dressed gentleman with a folded copy of *Race and Nation* in his hand. Go to him and ask him, 'Can you tell me how to get to the State Museum?' If he replies, 'Are you going to see Rembrandt's *Night Watch*?' he's the courier, and he'll lead you to the meeting place. Oh, one other thing! You're to bring somebody with you, a teacher by the name of John Van der Sloep."

Another surprise.

"How is that possible?" asked Uncle Henry. "How on earth did they learn your name way out in Amsterdam, John?"

"Hey, man," said William, "you're becoming known in high circles."

John didn't understand it either. He watched with disappointment as William left for the railway station by himself. But then when he sat down with Uncle Henry in the living room, suddenly he knew and his heart leaped at the thought. Who knew the alias on his I.D. better than the man who had made it? Father!

The Café Monopole was filled with German uniforms. By himself John wouldn't have had the nerve to enter the place. He followed Uncle Henry's broad back as he wound his way among the small tables, looking for an empty spot. As he did so, it dawned on him that this was an ideal meeting place. No one would expect underground workers to seek out the company of German officers.

You had to be able to put on the right face, however, and Uncle Henry was better at it than John. He hooked his thumb in his vest, stuck out his lower lip, and surveyed the room like a field marshal who has things well under control. He stirred his coffee as if it were a military manoeuvre. But when he took a sip of it, he momentarily lost his composure.

"Blah! Dishwater! Give me Aunt Nellie's coffee any day!" And he refused to take another swallow. In some ways they had it better than their conquerors.

At two minutes to three, a small, neatly dressed young man walked into the café with a rolled-up newspaper in his hand. He stood by the door scanning the restaurant and absent-mindedly tapping the paper against his shoulder. His eyes fell on Uncle Henry, and he slowly moved in his direction. John noticed an N.S.M. pin on the lapel of his coat. He was a good-looking fellow with the air of a young executive.

"Is this chair taken?" he asked.

"Depends," said Uncle Henry, looking him straight in the eye. "If you can tell us how to get to the State Museum, it's yours!"

"I'm afraid the *Night Watch* is gone," the young man said with a smile. "Shall we go? Vriend is my name."

John followed the two men across a busy square and down a tree-lined boulevard. He was enjoying the walk, even though it was a dark, rainy day. A short time ago he had been cooped up not far from here, afraid to show his face outside, day or night. Now he was strolling down the street free and easy. Each and every policeman had been ordered to arrest him, but he was free. He thrust out his chest and took a deep breath.

Vriend stopped in front of an apartment building on a quiet side street. They were supposed to go to the top floor, he said. Mr. Vriend rang and led them upstairs. Although it was quite dark on the landing, John immediately recognized the figure at the top of the stairs. He went flying by their guide and threw his arms around his waiting father.

"Am I glad to see you! Am I ever glad you could come!" Father said, looking him over and then hugging him again. "You're going to stay a couple of days, aren't you? Great! Then we'll have some time to talk."

"Ah-ha," said Uncle Henry. "Now I see what's what. He's a chip off the old block, Mr. Van der Sloep."

"Van Kampen," Father corrected him.

"Oh, alright. Everything's possible in these crazy times — even fathers and sons with different names. Where do we go?"

In a room overlooking the street, a dozen men sat around a table. John took a seat by one of the windows. Around the table were men from all walks of life: a farmer with a long-stemmed pipe; a gentleman with a Vandyke beard — he looked like a professor, thought John; a young man dressed as if he had come straight from the factory. At the head of the table sat a man with blond, curly hair. Sometimes he was addressed as "Reverend" and sometimes as "Fritz." So this man was the legendary "Fritz the Rover," one of the founders of the L.O. He had roamed from one end of the country to the other, exhorting people to resist.

These were the leaders of the underground, the generals of the secret army in which John, too, was a soldier. Among them sat Father, a little thinner than usual, and sporting a silvery mustache. Every so often Father's eyes rested on him, and a couple of times he threw John a quick wink. There was something different about him, something besides the mustache, and it made John uneasy.

The L.O. men congratulated Uncle Henry for the success of his group. From now on he would attend L.O. meetings and inform the committee of his plans, and then funnel ration cards out via L.O. couriers. The L.O. also agreed to help Uncle Henry support the men in his group; each man would get twenty guilders a week for room and board.

A woman entered the room with a tray full of teacups and the discussion trailed off for a while.

Sipping his tea, John looked down into the street. A young woman emerged from the apartment house across the street and eased her buggy down the steps. A stoop-shouldered man of about thirty, wearing round glasses and a beret, strolled beside the buggy. The husband? No, apparently not. Now he was passing the woman. He must have felt John's eyes on him, for he looked up at the windows.

In the room, someone was passing around copies of the latest issue of *Free Holland*, and John took one to read. At the end of the meeting, he gave the paper back to the man with the beard, and then waited by the window for Father. The mother across the street was slowly pulling the baby buggy up the

stoop, step by step. The man with the glasses and beret was also back. He must live in the neighbourhood, too. Or maybe not. He seemed to be lost — or looking for someone.

Father was finally free. They walked down the stairs with Uncle Henry but parted on the sidewalk. John once again had to promise to be back on the following Wednesday.

"Let's walk," suggested Father. "The streetcars are terribly crowded at this time of day, and the sun has come out."

John felt a wonderful sense of peace as he walked beside Father through the quiet summer evening. They stopped on a bridge and leaned on the parapet to watch a barge pass underneath, poled along by two men. The drops that fell from the ends of the poles caught the sun, glistening briefly like diamonds before splashing back into the water. A boy and girl strolled along the canal, arm in arm. The sound of a cooing dove carried across the water as if to say that here the world was not out of kilter, here goodness and happiness prevailed.

They stayed there long after the barge had disappeared. To John it seemed that no place was safer than the city. You could go where you pleased and no one paid any attention to you. Blending in with the thousands of faces on the street, you were hiding right in the open. For the first time in a long time, he had a sense of well-being that wasn't just a state of mind. It was . . .

He glanced at Father's face and got a sudden fright. There were tears in Father's eyes.

"What is it, Dad?" he asked anxiously.

"Oh, nothing. Nothing at all," Father said, trying to laugh. And he threw his arm around John's shoulders. "John, my boy, you have no idea how happy it makes me just to see you. What time is it, anyway? Almost seven? Then we've got to hurry. Someone's coming to see me at seven-thirty. Let's go!"

They walked on through the city, Father's arm still resting on John's shoulder.

CHAPTER SIX

In a narrow, quiet street Father stopped. Across the street was an old grocery store which had settled at a tilt and now leaned against the older but stronger warehouse next door. The front window was empty

except for a poster advertising Indonesian tea, which featured a beautiful Javanese woman in a colourful sarong.

"As long as that picture is hanging in the window, everything is okay," said Father. "So whenever you come to the house, look for the poster. The store is always locked, because it hasn't had anything to sell for over a year. The entrance is next door, number 17."

As soon as Father punched out the "V" signal on the doorbell, the door opened. They were greeted by a friendly middle-aged woman dressed in a very simple dress.

"Hi there, Sophie," said Father. "I'd like you to meet my son. You can call him John. Is it all right if we go straight upstairs?"

They went up to a small bedroom with flowered wallpaper. A double bed was folded up against the wall and covered with a curtain. Father opened the window for some fresh air. Then, as he poured some water into a bowl on the dresser, John looked out the window. Down below he saw a brown beret bobbing along the sidewalk, and then a flash of light on glasses. Was it the same fellow he had seen earlier? Not likely. That would be quite a coincidence in a city this size. Many people wore berets like that.

"Already you've got the mind of a resistance fighter," said Father with a smile. "Weren't you looking for another escape route? That's one drawback to this house. It has only one exit. The buildings on either side are quite a bit taller, so you can't escape over the roofs. But two excellent hiding places make up for the disadvantages. I'll show them to you in a couple of minutes."

When they had both washed up, he led John to a room in the rear of the house. A woman was sitting in bed doing embroidery. She strongly resembled the woman who had let them in, except that she was much paler and her hair was turning gray.

"Excuse me, Mrs. Steen," said Father. "This is my son, John. I'd like to show him our shelter, if it's all right with you."

He opened a clothes closet, which was full of clothes, reached down, and lifted a trap door in the bottom of the closet.

"One nice thing about these old eighteenth-century homes is that they have so many dead spaces," he said. "We can duck in here if it's very necessary and close the trap door from the other side. See? When those beams are slid through under here, this trap door is just as solid as the rest of the floor. It can't be lifted up. An air vent goes down into the space from the roof. We put a mattress down there and a little food. The room next to this one has a similar shelter. So we're ready for anything, right Mrs. Steen?"

The bedridden woman laughed and nodded. Chatting with her, John found out that she had been sick for ten years. But she wasn't an unhappy woman. On the contrary, she had a ready laugh, and she seemed not at all discontented. On the wall over her bed hung three texts, embroidered with flowers: "God is my Helper," "Put all your cares on Him," and "Praise the Lord, O my soul." Now she was busy with "Ask and it shall be given unto you." The "A" with all its loops and scrolls was almost finished.

"Well, what do you think of my handiwork?" she asked John, holding it up for his scrutiny. And John, of course, replied that it was beautiful, very well done, and he didn't see how she could make such tiny stitches. She beamed! No one had ever taught her anything about embroidery, she told him; she had picked it up entirely on her own. She had already sold 40 framed texts, and the money was for the resistance. Even though she was bedridden, she was helping in the fight against the Nazis!

In the dining room they were received by a tall, broad-shouldered old man whom everybody called Grandpa Meyer. He sat at the head of the table, a black skullcap on his white hair, and his hands folded in front of him on the table. Nine places were set at the table, and when "Aunt" Sophie struck a gong, people came spilling into the dining room from all corners of the house — a gray-haired Jewish couple, two Jewish girls in their mid-teens, obviously sisters, and a robust-looking fellow about John's age, who introduced himself as Ralph.

Grandpa Meyer led in prayer, talking to God as if He were sitting across from him at the table. On the wall over his bowed head was another of Mrs. Steen's texts. "Jesus shall overcome." Above the fireplace hung a picture of Queen Wilhelmina draped with orange ribbon.

After supper Sophie handed Grandpa Meyer a Bible. He opened it to Isaiah 54 and read as if the words were his own and he himself a prophet. Coming to the last verses, he paused and looked around the table, his eyes resting on John for a moment. Then he continued: *"No weapon that is fashioned against you shall prosper, and you shall confuse every tongue that rises against you in judgment. This is the heritage of the servants of the Lord and their vindication from Me, says the Lord."*

John was so impressed by the reading that when they were back in the small bedroom upstairs, he asked his father about the old man. Father told him that Grandpa read the passage from Isaiah once a week, especially if there was a new guest at the table.

"I have never before met a man with such a deep trust in God," said Father. "It's as if he feels invulnerable. Even if I brought the whole underground in here with me, it would be all right with him. Nothing is too much, and no one is turned away. He and his two daughters believe that the house is guarded by angels. And who knows?"

From downstairs came the sound of the doorbell. Ring-ring-ring-rrring! The "V" signal.

"That's for me," said Father. "Why don't you start writing a letter to Mother, and then I'll add a few lines later. She'll like that — to get a combined letter from us. Remember, no addresses."

John filled two pages on both sides, and then he wrote an even longer letter to Rita. He also penned a short letter to Uncle Gerrit. During these hours, Father came upstairs three times, and each time he was soon called down again by the familiar signal. A church clock in the neighbourhood had chimed ten when Father made his last trip upstairs.

He sighed wearily. "Tomorrow we'll get out of here," he promised. "I know a good spot where none of our comrades will be able to find us. We can be by ourselves for a while."

He switched off the light and opened the blackout curtain. Then they sat down by the open window. High overhead, squadrons of English and American bombers bored through the blackness of the night on their way to the industrial centres of Germany. The pale fingers of searchlights clawed impotently at the heavens.

They heard Grandpa come bumping up the stairs and then intoning his evening prayers on the other side of the thin wall that separated them. They closed the curtains again, switched on the light, and also got ready for bed. John studied his father. He looked sallow with exhaustion, and when he tossed his head back to swallow a pill, he almost lost his balance.

"You on medication?" John asked.

Father took a swallow of water, grimaced, and then laughed. "No, I'm okay. It's just a sleeping pill."

"You're too busy."

"Oh . . . perhaps. Why don't you sleep next to the wall? Then I won't wake you if I get up. Sometimes I go and sit by the window for a while if I can't get to sleep right away."

They lay side by side, talking quietly in the stillness of the night. They talked about Mother and the children, especially about Fritz. He was a constant worry to Mother, for, young as he was, he was already doing errands for the resistance. As always, he was very bold and reckless. And they talked about John's work with Uncle Henry's group. And about life after the war, when they would once again be able to live together in peace. They would rebuild their home in the country and live as they had before, without fear or danger. They would once more be able to go where they wanted and say what was on their minds. They would be free again! Yes, free . . . They had almost forgotten what it was like. As he tried to imagine the future, John's eyes filled with tears of longing and grief, confusion and despair, hope and joy.

"Have you ever thought that we might never see it?" Father asked him after a long silence. "We may not make it to the end, John. Not everyone who fights for freedom will see it."

John didn't answer. He couldn't. His throat seemed to have pinched shut at the thought that Father might not be with them at the end of the war.

"That's why I wanted you to stay with Uncle Herman," Father's voice continued. "Yes, I know that was hard on you. But what if I could find you another place, where you had something to do? Like a farm or something . . . You still awake, John?"

"Yes, Dad."

They lay side by side listening to each other's breathing.

"But *your* life is more important to Mother than mine is, Dad. *You* should stop! You're working yourself to a frazzle. Or at least you should get away for a while. You need some peace and rest!"

Again silence. Father heaved a deep sigh.

"Well, am I right?" insisted John.

"Perhaps you are," Father conceded. "Sometimes I think this life is driving me crazy. It's not just the work, it's also the fear and uncertainty. And worrying about Mother and the rest of you. The most frightening thing is that the work keeps expanding; it's so hard to say no, because there are always human lives involved.

Stop? I'm afraid that's impossible, John. Not only *can't* I quit. I also don't *want* to. No one can, once he's been drawn into this work. If I went into hiding now, I'd soon be climbing the walls. You know what I mean?"

"Yes," said John. "That's what happened to me when I was at Uncle Herman's."

"I was glad to hear it," said Father. But then he corrected himself, "or maybe, I *should* have been glad to hear it, but I wasn't. It meant I might lose you. I couldn't stand the thought of that, John. You're still so young. You've still got your whole life ahead of you."

A note of hopelessness had crept into Father's voice, and John recalled Father's face at the bridge that afternoon. He reached out for him in the darkness, and had to struggle to control his voice.

"You worry too much about other people," he told Father. "If you promise not to worry about me, I'll promise not to worry about you. Then each of us can look after himself. That would save us both a lot of worries, right? Remember, you're a worrywart!"

That was one of the names Mother called Father when he used to pace about the house. John heard Father chuckle. He was over his moment of despair.

"Yes, John, this fight is worth giving our lives for. We're fighting for one of the most important things in the world — freedom of conscience! But one of us *must* survive, John, to take care of Mother and the children!"

"One of us must survive." John was still mulling over those words when the clock in the church steeple spilled twelve pure notes into the night.

He had barely dozed off, it seemed, when Father was shaking him. Someone was pounding and shouting, and the doorbell was ringing on and on.

"Wake up, John! It's a raid! The Germans are here. Come on! Hurry!"

Father raised the bed up against the wall and pulled the curtain over it. Then he checked his revolver and slipped it into the pocket of his housecoat. "Grab your bag and clothes, and follow me!"

The hall was full of people running in both directions. The girls, groggy with sleep, were being hauled along by Ralph and Sophie. The elderly couple hurried by, arm in arm, the woman moaning with fear. Grandpa, still tying his housecoat, was going downstairs to answer the door. Mrs. Steen was stumbling about the bedroom, reciting her most recent text: "Ask and it shall be given unto you."

The closet was standing open, and the black hole of the trap door yawned up from the floor. First the old couple! But the old woman got stuck in the opening. Halfway through, she was afraid to let herself drop because she felt nothing under her feet. She screamed with terror, then finally let go.

The old man was quicker. And then John was tossing his bag and clothes into the hole. As he landed, Father fell on top of him. But he jumped up again, pulling the trap door shut, and slid the beams in place. If only Mrs. Steen remembered to close the closet door! John felt a mattress, a biscuit tin, and then the legs of the old woman. She was still moaning.

"Put your hand over her mouth," Father whispered. "I'll stay by the trap door." But her husband was already with her. "Be quiet, Wife!" he whispered. "Be quiet! O Lord of hosts . . ."

John nudged him aside and laid the woman down on the mattress. He felt a pillow under his hand and picked it up, holding it ready to put over the woman's face, if necessary. But now she was still. She, too, must have heard that the Germans were inside. Heavy boots were trampling all over the house. A thump, and then the sound of breaking glass.

"You lie, you lie!" a hoarse voice shouted in German. It was a cry of rage. Doors slammed open and shut. A couple of men came storming up the stairs. John could feel the floor vibrating under him. His only fear was that the woman would begin moaning again. He still held the pillow ready. Now the soldiers were in the bedroom, not more than six feet away. They pounded their rifle butts against the walls and the floor.

"Where are they?" a voice bellowed.

All they heard of Mrs. Steen's answer was the word "sick." The rest was drowned out by the stomping of boots. The closet door squeaked. Hands probed and tapped the wall. John flinched as a rifle butt hammered directly overhead on the trap door. Then it was quiet. The footsteps retreated. Their hiding place had not been discovered! Mrs. Steen was dragged downstairs. But there were other soldiers upstairs. John could hear them talking in another room.

"Somebody slept here! The bed's still warm."

"They're in here somewhere, those scum! We'll find them." The latter was the voice of a Dutchman. So there was a traitor with the Germans, helping them search out and capture his own people. And he seemed to know what he was doing. He had found the shelter in the other room. John could hear him shouting at the others to come out. He laughed triumphantly as the two whimpering girls were chased downstairs.

Suddenly John heard the scuffling sound of feet and a loud thud on the wall. Then the turncoat was swearing shrilly. Ralph must be putting up a fight!

But soon he was being clubbed and kicked down the stairs. Every sound carried to the shelter where John and Father were hiding, so they could follow exactly what was happening. John bit his lower lip

as he tried to control himself. They had only one revolver! They couldn't do anything against all those
soldiers. To try to help the others would be insane.
They could only keep quiet and wait.

John discovered that he was covered with sweat
from head to foot. Even his hair was wet. From fear?
But he hadn't really felt afraid — only a raw ache in
the middle of his chest as if something was about to
burst. He could hear muffled sounds from downstairs
— a scream, vibrations, more raucous laughter. Then
a voice high with pain: "Stop, stop, please! I don't
know — really, I don't!"

"Those fiends!" Father said, half aloud. Suddenly
the old woman began moaning again, but John
quickly smothered the sound with the pillow. Then,
for a long time, they heard nothing from downstairs,
until from the street came the deep growl of a truck
engine that stopped in front of the house. By the
sound of it, the others were being led outside and
loaded onto the truck. Were they taking the sickly
Mrs. Steen, too? A door slammed, and the engine
revved up again. Were they all gone?

They listened, holding their breath. Something
was still stirring downstairs! The scrape of a chair
being moved, the squeak of a door hinge. Someone
cleared his throat. With horrible certainty they realized that they were still far from safe. Someone had
stayed behind to occupy the house. But for how long?
It was getting stifling hot in the small space, and
the air was already turning stale. Maybe the air vent
was plugged. John groped along the wall, looking
for the vent. It was behind Father, who was leaning
against it.

The opening was quite small; the vent seemed to
have been made from a stovepipe. A wad of paper
had been shoved into the opening. Still there from
winter perhaps. He pulled it out and held his mouth

in front of the hole, taking several deep breaths. Then he felt around until he found his clothes. Quietly he pulled on his pants over his pyjamas. Then he sat down on the foot of the mattress. The old woman was quiet. She seemed to be sleeping. The old man was sitting beside her, softly reciting a Jewish prayer.

"No weapon that is fashioned against you shall prosper!" With what certainty and triumph the old man had pronounced those words. But now he was caught! Maybe he was already locked up in a cell, or maybe he was being tortured for information. Where were the angels who were supposed to be guarding the house? Or had there never been any? What did those words from Isaiah mean?

John stretched out his leg to ease a cramp in his thigh, and his foot hit the slanted wall of the shelter. "Shh!" said Father. John held his breath, listening, but he heard only the pounding of his heart. His head felt as if it were stuffed with cotton. He took a couple of deep breaths and felt a little better. He closed his eyes and leaned back against the wall.

Suddenly he was startled wide awake by the sound of the doorbell. The clock in the steeple struck four. From downstairs came the sound of voices and laughter. Then footsteps sounded on the stairs. Had someone given them away? John could hear Father moving back toward the trap door. In his mind, John could see the pistol in his hands. Two men came tramping down the hall. No, they weren't coming to this room. Were they going to start searching again?

"The old man had some goods stashed away. Stinking old hoarder! We might as well take some. He won't be back. I wonder if he had any wine stashed away."

"Maybe downstairs in the store. Or in the cellar," answered another voice. "Look! Over here. This is where they were hiding. Two young broads and a young tough, dodging the labour draft. He started swinging like a crazy fool, caught me by surprise, and gave me a bloody nose. But he'll get it back with interest, you can be sure of that! We were really after somebody else. An older man with a gray mustache. But he'd flown the coop. He was here last night. They saw him go in! But he's a slippery customer. Probably got wind of it."

One of them cleared his throat and spat on the floor.

"Fools!" said the voice. "Some hiding place! What do they take us for? Idiots? Look at that trap door! My boy could do better. Just yesterday I was saying, 'It's almost impossible to hide yourself in a house so that you can't be found,' but most people don't know how to search. You tap the walls, and right away you can tell where it's hollow. Did you tap all the walls in the whole house?"

"Of course. What do you think? I'm not some greenhorn. You want to double check?"

"What? You kidding? I'm not here to check on your work. I know you're experienced! Can you understand why an old man like that risks his life for a bunch of lousy Jews?"

"Not me. He had guts though, that old-timer! At the station the captain put a gun to his head, and you know what the old geezer said? 'Go ahead. I'd be proud to die for God's people.' And he said it just as calmly as if he were telling you the time."

"Well, by now he probably *knows* what time it is — his last hour," said the other with a laugh. "He'll get his chance to die proud. That Webber is a real devil!"

"Of course, the old fellow doesn't have much to lose, either. I'm sure he's well over eighty. Come on, let's see if we can find his cellar."

They went clattering back down the stairs. Father quietly lowered himself to the floor.

"Maybe there *is* an angel watching over us," thought John.

The old woman slept on, exhausted by fear. She probably hadn't even heard the two men come up-stairs. Her husband was once again reciting prayers under his breath, and occasionally he uttered a quiet groan. When John bumped his foot, he fell silent. There was a buzzing in John's ears, like the sound of a light drizzle on the roof. And it was getting hard for him to breathe. He gradually sank into semi-con-sciousness, coming to now and again with a start, sure that he'd been talking out loud. In between, he heard the clock in the church steeple mark off every hour and half hour — five chimes for five o'clock, one for five-thirty . . .

It would be getting light outside by now; the sun would be rising over the city. A trolley rumbled by outside. Soon there were more noises — the ringing of a bicycle bell, the hoot of a factory whistle, auto-mobile sounds, and the clatter of handcarts, the shouts of children. The city had awakened and was going on with life as usual.

Did the people outside realize how wonderful it was just to be able to go about their daily routine? John wiped the sweat from his face with his pyja-mas sleeve, which was already drenched with sweat. His throat ached with thirst, but there was no water in the shelter. Why hadn't they thought of that? He thought of the tin of biscuits, but, no, he would never get one down his parched throat.

At eight o'clock there was a changing of the guard. Again, a couple of men came clumping up the stairs to look at the hiding place that had been found. The new men began going into other rooms and tapping on the walls and floors. Father and John stood with their backs pressed against the wall of the closet in case they also sounded that wall. That would deaden the sound. But the men seemed to go through every room except Mrs. Steen's. The angel was still there.

Then, once more, it was sit and wait, wait and sweat, wait and think about the burning thirst, wait and listen to the steeple clock tolling out the hours. How long would this last? When would the men leave?

The doorbell. Ring-ring-ring-rrring! The "V" signal!

The "V" signal? A resistance worker! He apparently didn't know what had happened during the night and was walking into a trap. Had Grandpa or the girls not had the chance to take the poster out of the shop window? Father grabbed John's arm and squeezed until it hurt. They heard the front door opening, a shout, and the sounds of a struggle. Then quiet. The Germans had made a catch. Later they heard loud voices and screams of pain coming from the dining room as their comrade was interrogated.

"I can't take this any longer!" Father whispered hoarsely. "I've got to get downstairs and take down that poster!"

A spasm of fear passed through John, leaving him faint and nauseous. With trembling hands he seized Father and pulled him toward himself.

"You can't!" John whispered. "To get to the store you have to go right by the dining room, and that's where they are. You won't make it!"

"I've got to try! If this keeps up, they'll catch everybody." Father tried to pull himself loose, but John only tightened his grip.

"It's crazy!" he whispered desperately. "They'll get you for sure, and then you'll have led them to us too. Then we're *all* goners. You're not going!"

"I won't tell them anything. If you put the beams back after I . . ."

"No! Remember our agreement?" They were both panting, and Father seemed to be weakening. "One of us must survive. For Mother and . . ." Father went limp under John's hands, and he slumped down on the end of the mattress. His breath was coming in strange sobs. Was he weeping? Good. That would do him good. John put his arm around Father's shoulder and hugged him tightly. Father's shirt was dripping wet.

"I've got to stay with him," thought John. "I can't go back to Uncle Henry. Sometimes Dad is just like Fritz and charges in blindly without a thought of danger. If I stay with him, maybe I can see to it that he doesn't overwork himself. Maybe I can even take over part of the load."

He was making plans as if he were sure that they would make it out of here. And suddenly, in the depths of his heart, he was sure of it, absolutely sure! It was only for a moment, however, but that moment of certainty gave him strength. In a sudden vision he had seen himself and Father walking down a street together and entering a house. A memory flash from yesterday? Or a sign of tomorrow — perhaps from their guardian angel?

The hours stretched out infinitely and then seemed to collapse into each other. Again and again, the well-known signal was tapped out on the doorbell, and each time a struggle followed at the door and another comrade was interrogated in a mélange of screams and curses. Father seemed to have given up the idea of getting out. He lay stretched out on the floor, limp and unmoving. Once in a while John heard him sigh deeply. But shortly after the doorbell had rung for the sixth time — twice it had been an ordinary ring, not the "V" signal — they both suddenly jumped up. The house exploded with noise, breaking glass, crashing chairs, running feet, shouts, and a couple of shots. John and Father whispered excitedly, trying to guess what had happened. An escape attempt? Had resistance fighters come to rescue them? Or had someone tried to get the poster out of the window?

They finally settled on the latter. For soon it was quiet again downstairs, and another truck drove up to carry off the prisoners. It didn't make sense for the Germans to stay anymore. At least, not if they understood the meaning of the poster.

But they did stay, for John heard the pounding of a hammer downstairs. And a short while later someone was whistling in the kitchen as he washed dishes. By now it was well into the afternoon, and the air was getting so bad that they had to take turns standing at the air vent. The woman, however, slept on or else had lapsed into unconsciousness. When the clock in the steeple struck three, Father quietly opened the trap door, which seemed to help. John felt himself breathing more easily. But it was only for a little while, for a new shift arrived and Father hastened to close the hatch again. They had a momentary fright as the beams jammed and then squeaked as they were forced into place. The humidity must have caused the wood to expand. The walls of the enclosure were wet with their breath.

They listened anxiously as feet came thumping up the stairs once more. Again, Nazis tramped from room to room, laughing and talking. John caught himself thinking that if they were found, at least he would get fresh air and a drink of water.

He was shocked at his own thoughts and scolded himself, "Don't be crazy! You can take it. People have gotten out of much tighter spots. Just think of Uncle Gerrit under the floor of the burning house. That wasn't any picnic either!" After the Germans had gone back downstairs, John again carefully opened the trap door and eagerly stuck his head outside to get a breath of fresh air. But the closet door had been shut and there was no knob on the inside. They would have to break the lock when the police were gone. When the police were gone? When would they go?

Father tugged at his arm and guided him to the air vent. "Here, it's your turn!" He lasted only a couple of minutes, and then his knees buckled and he let himself slide to the floor along the wet wall. The woman had awakened and Father and the old man wrestled her to her feet to get her to the air vent. That was the last thing he remembered before he drifted off into a stupor.

"The bell hasn't rung anymore since . . ." Who was talking? He tried to rouse himself. He wanted to tell Father that the bell hadn't rung since . . . since . . . But he had lost it. A kaleidoscope of images passed before his eyes. He was out in the pasture with Fritz, and they were trying to raise a kite. The ground was wet with rain, and his heels sank into the soil. Then he was sitting across from Rita in a café in Rotterdam. She lifted her glass to him and smiled. But as he lifted his glass, he found himself in Aunt Nellie's living room standing with the group around the table. They were singing the national anthem. On the table before him was a beef sandwich and a large glass of cold milk, but he couldn't eat or drink until the song was finished. And the song went on and on, with crazy Leo beating out the rhythm on his head.

The hammering on his head went on as someone shook him awake. "Shhh! John, are you crazy? What a time to start singing. Are you asleep? John! Do you hear me, John?"

"Hmm — Hmmmm," said John, finally realizing where he was. "Did I fall asleep?" he asked softly.

"Yes, several hours . . . Now be quiet! They're . . . changing shifts again.

Father gasped out the words. John noticed that he was wheezing himself. They couldn't last much longer. Something had to happen pretty soon. Again there were words and laughter, but this time they sounded as if they were in his head, and his head echoed like an empty washtub. He clutched his ears with his hands. Father tugged him up and pushed him in front of the vent. He stood there awhile and then let himself slide back down to the floor. Just as he was nodding off again, footsteps echoed on the stairs. Father quickly pulled the trap door shut.

This time it was only one man, and he walked very quietly. He went down the hall and came right into Mrs. Steen's room. They heard the click of the light switch and then the squeak of the closet door. Suddenly John was wide awake; he quickly pulled himself to his feet and stood next to Father.

"There's only one of them," he thought. "We can take him, if Father doesn't shoot right away. Otherwise, the two downstairs will come running."

Then there was a soft tapping on the bottom of the closet. Tap, tap, tap, TAP.

The "V" signal! Had someone come to save them? Or had they been betrayed? Was it a trick to get them to come out?

"Anybody there?" a voice whispered urgently. "Please answer . . . This is Hermans, Officer Hermans. I've come to help."

"Thank God!" said Father, and quickly loosened the hatch. John saw the head of a man with a police cap, which quickly pulled back.

"Come on, hurry!" the policeman whispered. "Careful, or they'll hear you downstairs. How could you stand it so long in there? The air almost makes me sick up here!"

They all had to push and pull on the old woman to get her out, and then she collapsed on the bed, weeping quietly. John was the last one to come out. He wobbled and had to lean against the wall. But the air was like cool water, and John drank it in greedily. The officer gave them a few minutes to recover and put on the rest of their damp clothes. Then, shoes in hand, they followed him quietly into the hall and down the stairs.

There was still a German in the house, but the other policeman was distracting him. They could hear his loud chatter very clearly as they tiptoed down the hall, single file. Father was carrying his automatic in his hand. Now that freedom lay just ahead, fear of failure was sharper in John than it had been during the whole ordeal. But the front door opened noiselessly in front of them, and the officer pushed them out, giving them each a slap on the back as they passed through the door. Outside, they were seized by other hands and led down the sidewalk. In the group was a young girl. She smiled at John. "You're a fortunate fellow," she said.

"Yes," said John, "you can say that again!" How inadequate words seemed to him at that moment.

"Grandpa and his two daughters are in the prison on Amstelveen Road," she told him. "And so are the two girls and Ralph. I'm afraid they're all goners. The Germans in the house grabbed four of our boys this morning. But Sophie managed to get a message out of prison through a guard. So then Vriend rushed over here and smashed the window with a brick to knock down the poster. The Germans took a couple of shots at him, but they missed."

"Vriend? The courier? That little man?" asked John. "We thought . . ." Suddenly panic seized him, and he halted, looking around wildly. "Dad!" he shouted.

But then a hand pushed him forward. "I'm right behind you. Don't worry! Everything's all right. Keep walking. Don't talk so much out on the street, Jeanette. Wait till we get home."

They had made it! They were again walking down the street together. They had both survived! Occasionally the group met someone on the sidewalk. It was so dark on the street that sometimes they almost collided with others. John wondered how his rescuers found their way so confidently through the almost impenetrable blackness, for he was completely lost.

The old woman, who was walking somewhere ahead of John, suddenly began giggling, and she couldn't stop. When they finally turned and entered a building, she was still giggling. Not until after she had been set down in an easy chair and given a glass of water did her giggles stop. And then they turned into sobs. She was completely overwrought.

A glassful of clear, cold water, unbelievably wet and cool. And then another one! Sandwiches and coffee. And Father's pale, unshaven face, and eyes red-rimmed but happy when they looked at him — profoundly and everlastingly happy.

Down the table from Father sat the neat, fragile-looking Mr. Dick Vriend, who had actually tried to snatch the poster after smashing the window. He had managed to get only the bottom half of it. Another young fellow held it up as if it were a captured flag. Dick was barraged with wisecracks about his heroism. But Dick didn't join in the laughter.

"Okay, fellows, lay off now. I've been wracking my brain all afternoon trying to figure out how they found out about that house. Now, you say they came especially for *you*," he said, turning to Father. "Do you understand it?"

"Afraid not," said Father.

But John suddenly saw in front of him the brown beret and the flash of glasses! At some point during their long ordeal in the shelter, he had become sure that the strange, bespectacled figure had been following them. Had he dreamed it? Everything was still confused in his mind; it was still hard for him to think coherently. But he told his story anyway. When John was finished, Dick slammed his palm on the table and swore that he would nail the traitor.

"Would you recognize him if you saw him again?" he asked John.

"I think so," said John.

"Then tomorrow you and I are going into town," Dick said. "And if necessary, the next day, and the next. He's probably still snooping around. I wouldn't be surprised if we ran into him somewhere. It can't have been a coincidence that he showed up first at the south address and then at Grandpa Meyer's."

"You think it's worthwhile to go looking for him? It would be like looking for a needle in a haystack," said Father, eyeing John anxiously.

He's worried about me again, John thought to himself. "Of course it's worth the try!" said John. "If we *don't* get him, it won't be safe for any of you to carry on your work here anymore."

"And who knows how many people he's got his eye on at other places," added Dick. "He may have been following you for days! John, I'll pick you up at eight o'clock tomorrow morning. We'll just hope that he is wearing the same outfit. You point him out to me, and I'll take care of the rest!"

Once again John and Father slept in the same bed, but this time it was a luxurious bed with linen sheets in a large bedroom with a crystal chandelier and a washbasin for each of them. Father stood in front of one of the mirrors, shaving off his mustache. Their host and his wife had moved to the children's bedroom for the night, giving their own bedroom to the exhausted father and son. But tonight Grandpa Meyer and his daughters were sleeping on hard bunks — or on the floor — in a prison along Amstelveen Road.

At eight o'clock the next morning Dick Vriend was knocking at the door. He was wearing sneakers, which somehow made him look even smaller than he was. Dick and John spent the entire day sauntering up and down the streets, eyeing people. John had never before realized how many people wore brown berets. They scrutinized the lines in front of all the theatres and jostled through the crowds at the market; they checked along the boulevards where the upper class lived and in the narrow lanes of the slum neighbourhoods. John learned more about Amsterdam in one day than any other farm boy from the north had ever done. But at the end of the day, he had nothing to show for all his efforts except two blistered and weary feet.

The next day he began to doubt whether he would recognize the man even if he *did* see him. Maybe he had already passed the fellow on the street without recognizing him. What had been the colour of his shirt — brown or beige? And he probably changed it by now. Was he as small as he had seemed to be from the upstairs window? And maybe the round glasses had been part of a disguise. And, of course, he might be wearing a hat or a cap by now, instead of a beret. John confessed his doubts to Dick Vriend as they sat over a beer in a small café, but Dick dismissed them with a peremptory wave of his hand.

"Don't be giving up yet," he said. "We've got to get that traitor! I don't care *what* he's wearing! You saw him three times, and you'll recognize him — by his walk, his posture, the total impression he makes. You'll feel it in your guts when you see him, because you hate him for his treachery. Just wait and see! I've done this sort of thing before."

So they went on, up one street and down the next. They covered the neighbourhood around the house where the L.O. meeting had taken place. Dick had heard that this place had also been raided, but that the Germans had found nothing. When the people were asked why they'd had so many visitors the day before, they explained that it had been a birthday party. And a check of their I.D.'s showed that it had indeed been the man's birthday the preceding day.

As John lay in bed that night, he calculated that if they let all the people in Amsterdam pass in review at the rate of one per second for twelve hours a day, it would take them twenty days. However, he still went along with Dick Vriend the next day and kept his eyes open. By now he had little hope of finding the man. At noon Dick took him to his home for dinner, and even there he put John at a window where he could keep an eye on the street.

Toward evening they gathered their courage and decided to make a pass down the street past Grandpa Meyer's little store in the absurd hope that maybe the criminal would return to the scene of his crime, as in mystery novels. The store window had been boarded up, and all the curtains were pulled shut. Looking up at the second story, John once more breathed a prayer of thanks for his miraculous escape.

Then they meandered into the south end of the city. The sky was turning red, and wisps of fog were starting to rise from the canals. It would be a dark night again tonight. A green car, mottled with camouflage, slowly passed them and turned the corner ahead. They followed it and saw it stop in front of the local S.D. headquarters. Two uniformed men got out, pulled a civilian out of the back seat, and dragged him up the steps into the building. Then the car drove off again.

"Another victim," Dick said bitterly.

"Stop!" said John. "Wait a minute!"

Out of the door of the building into which the S.D. and their victim had just disappeared, came a slight, stoop-shouldered man. He stopped on the steps for a moment to talk to a German officer. Then he shook hands, gave the Hitler salute, and hurried down the street.

"That's him!" John whispered excitedly.

"Are you sure?" asked Dick.

"Positive! Just look at him — the same beret, a brown shirt, and he's wearing glasses. See, he's just turning his head!"

They followed the man as he turned right at the next corner and headed toward the centre of the city.

"Not much to look at," murmured Dick. "I'm sure he was rejected by the German army, and now he's getting his kicks playing spy. You're *sure* it's him? Give me your word!"

"I swear that it's the same man I saw three times the day before the raid," said John.

"Alright, I believe you," answered Dick. "In any case, only a rotten traitor would be so buddy-buddy with the S.D. You can find your own way back to-night, can't you? Thanks for your help."

"I'm not leaving," said John.

"Yes, you are!"

"Listen, Dick, I can't just let you tackle him alone!"

Dick snapped, "You think I need help with a lousy little runt like that? You stay here! That's an order!"

Dick accelerated his pace, and John stopped. But when Dick had pulled half a block ahead of him, he followed anyway. Around a corner to the right they went, across the street, turning left, and then down a street intersected by a large canal. It was getting darker, so John had to close the distance between himself and Dick in order to keep him in sight.

When Dick reached the corner by the canal, John wasn't far behind. John stopped at the corner. This was the spot, he felt instinctively. There were no people here, and the canal was lined with warehouses. A gray curtain of fog rose from the canal, shrouding the trees along its banks. The man in the beret and glasses — only a dark shadow now — angled across the road, walking quickly toward the bridge. Dick

followed close behind, his sneakers soundless on the pavement. Two slight shadows disappeared into the fog.

John suddenly found himself hurrying, almost running, in the opposite direction. He wanted to get away as fast as possible. But even before he had reached the end of the block, a shot reverberated through the black city streets.

CHAPTER SEVEN

As he approached Aunt Nellie's house through the back garden on Wednesday evening, John heard voices coming from an open window. So most of the group was back already! His heart warmed; in the last few days he had begun to realize how attached he was to his second family.

In the living room he was greeted with a guarded cheer.

"Hey, John! Welcome back, Johnny! Where's your lady?"

"Lady?"

"Yes. We were supposed to find a girl to act as a courier, remember? Did you find one?"

"Well, if necessary, Rita will come," said John. "It will be up to Uncle Henry."

Another cheer went up.

"That's four, Henry!" they said. "We'd better organize a special women's squad. See how seriously we take your assignments?"

"Four?" asked John.

"Sure," said Joe. "I found a girl who'd be willing to come, just like yours. But Leo and Ev — or rather, Robert — each brought one *along*. The ladies are upstairs getting dressed for the party. Uncle Henry wants to keep *both* of them. He says there's plenty of work for two. Otherwise, one of them can give Aunt Nellie a hand. Here they are! Ladies, let me introduce you to John Van der Sloep, teacher on furlough — at least, according to his I.D. John, Sylvia and Angie, the latest additions to the family."

John shook hands with each girl. Angie gave him a warm grip. She appeared to be a frank and friendly country girl, although she acted a little shy. Sylvia held out a cool, languid hand, sized him up with a brief

glance, and then lowered long lashes over her big, dark eyes.

John couldn't take his eyes off her. When had he seen such a beautiful face? Ivory skin, thin eyebrows, and her full, red lips — everything to perfection. As the girls took their places around the table, John noticed that the eyes of all the other fellows were on Sylvia. She seemed to have impressed everybody, including Uncle Henry.

Now Robert began to give her qualifications. Apparently he wanted to make it clear that he hadn't brought her along just for her pretty face.

"Go ahead, Sylvia," he urged her. "Tell them about the jailbreak. It's something we can all learn from."

"Well," said Sylvia, "there was really nothing to it. Anybody here could have done the same thing." Her voice was low and controlled, and her eyes moved around the table with a detached look. "I was part of a group that had established a secret radio station we called 'The Voice of Freedom.' We broadcasted twice a week: Wednesday and Saturday evenings right after Radio Orange. We wanted to inform the people about what was really going on in the country and to arouse them enough to resist."

"The Voice of Freedom?" exclaimed Joe. "Then I heard you sometimes. Boy, were you ever fierce!"

"The fiercer, the better," Sylvia said calmly. "Sometimes it takes a lot to wake people up. You know that, I'm sure. First we had the transmitter in a house in Amstelveen. Later we moved it to a houseboat that we anchored behind a small island in the marshes by Loosdrecht. But we were forced to leave when the Germans triangulated our location. We saw the patrols looking for us on the shore, but we managed to slip out with the boat just in the nick of time.

"Next we anchored in the vicinity of Vinkeveen. We thought we'd be safe there for a while, but either the Germans had seen us when we were escaping or someone betrayed us. In the middle of our first broadcast from the new location, they jumped us. I was at the microphone when they burst in, so I was in deep. But I never gave up, and I never told them anything I didn't want them to know."

"Did they hurt you?" asked Robert.

"They never laid a hand on me," said Sylvia. "But once they interrogated me for twenty hours at a stretch with a bright light blazing right in my eyes. They worked in shifts. I don't suppose you'd call that torture . . ."

"Not if driving a person crazy isn't torture!" exclaimed William indignantly. And there was a murmur of agreement from the others.

"You didn't tell them anything?" asked Uncle Henry.

"Nothing important," she said, studying her nail polish. She looked up from under her lashes and continued, "But I was fortunate. In my purse was a letter, signed 'Bob,' who had asked me to meet him on Friday, four-thirty, at a railway station in The Hague. It was an old letter, and we had already met. But fortunately it was undated, and the fact that the letter might be old never seemed to occur to the S.D. I let it slip that the meeting involved the leader of our group, who had been air-dropped into the country from England. So, of course, they were determined to get their hands on him.

"They decided that I should keep the appointment — with them looking on, of course. They threatened me with all kinds of reprisals if I tried to warn the man before they could capture him. Two S.D. officers drove me to the railway station in The Hague. They parked the car beside the station and accompanied me onto the platform. I was ordered to wait on the platform while they watched from either side, their hands on their guns.

"At four-thirty nobody showed up, of course. I could see that they were starting to get suspicious, and I still didn't know what I was going to do. But then, on the opposite platform I saw a man with a briefcase under his arm. He was just getting ready to board a train. I didn't know him, but I pretended he was the man I was to meet. 'Hello, Bob!' I shouted. 'Over here! I'm over here!' My S.D. guards jumped off the platform and went running across the tracks to grab the stranger. Suddenly the man turned and ran. That gave me the chance to make my escape. While they were chasing this stranger, shouting and shooting, I calmly walked out of the station, and here I am."

"Tell them about the car, Sylvia," urged Robert.

"Oh, do I have to?" she protested. "I don't want to sit here talking about myself all night. What will your friends think?"

But of course they all urged her to go on with her story, and so she continued, "Well, I got outside, I saw the car standing there — the one in which they had driven me to the station. So I thought, why not take it along? I had driven that make before. So that's what I did."

"You mean they left the key in it?" asked John.

"Pardon?" she said, looking at John.

"Of course," said Robert impatiently. "How else could she drive it? Go on, Sylvia."

"Well, there's nothing else to tell. I drove it to Rotterdam, where I've got a girlfriend. And then I didn't know what to do with the car, so I drove it into the canal, and as far as I know it's still there."

"How'd you do that?" John asked, amazed at the daring of this fragile looking girl. "Did you put it in first gear? And how did you hold down the gas pedal? Or was it downhill?"

"Well, how do you drive a car into the water?" said Sylvia. "I may not know much about the technical part of cars, but I knew how to do that. You just drive straight ahead and jump out at the last minute — that's all."

Robert continued the story. "She went into hiding at her girlfriend's house, which is where I found her last week. She was ready to join a group in Rotterdam, but I thought, 'That's just the kind of girl we need!' So I said to her, 'You'd be better off working in another part of the country for a while. Why don't you come with us? We can use a courageous young lady like you.' Right, Uncle Henry?"

"I should think so," Uncle Henry said absentmindedly, looking at the clock.

She had stretched her story a bit, John thought. To drive a car into a canal wasn't all that easy. But . . . she was still quite a gal!

Her eyes met his for a moment, and he was startled at their coldness. Did she sense that he doubted her story?

"Okay, Angie. Now it's your turn," said Leo, nudging her.

"Me?" asked Angie self-consciously. "Go on! I've got nothing much to tell. My life's never been in danger or anything scary like that. All I've ever done was bring around papers and ration cards and stuff. And I was helping to hide people — Jews and other divers — and then one man that we were hiding got found, and he snitched on a whole bunch of the others. So my dad thought maybe I should make myself scarce for a while. So when he" — she nodded at Leo — "came along and talked to my dad about you needing somebody to carry messages and stuff . . ."

"And we'll have plenty of work for both of you," promised Uncle Henry. "We've got some interesting jobs in the works. You'll see!"

"I came across a distribution centre that's just ripe for picking," an-nounced William.

"And I know of an N.S.M. hall where hundreds of weapons are stored," Leo added excitedly. "If we could get our hands on those — man-oh-man! Listen . . ."

The time flew by as they discussed various possibilities. Uncle Henry sat by silently, and soon some of the others began to steal glances at the clock. Finally it was quarter to eleven. Aunt Nellie and Angie were setting the table, and Pete still hadn't showed up.

"If he isn't here at eleven, he isn't coming," said Leo.

"And then you can be sure that something is wrong," said Uncle Henry. "As a matter of fact, I'm sure of it already!"

"Oh, come on, chief," protested Robert. "Pete may not be the swiftest, but he's not one to go looking for trouble. He looks before he leaps; in fact, he looks and looks and looks."

"Maybe his child or his wife is sick, so he stayed on a few days longer," suggested Joe. "And while we sit here worrying, he's sleeping in a nice, soft bed."

"So you think he went home?" asked Uncle Henry.

"Where else would he go?" asked Joe. "That's all he ever thought about. You couldn't have kept him away from his family with a team of horses!"

Aunt Nellie came in carrying a huge bouquet of flowers for a centrepiece, and Angie followed her with a tray of wine glasses. Aunt Nellie hadn't only roasted a piece of beef, she had prepared a feast! But no one felt like celebrating; everyone was acutely aware that one of the family was missing. During the meal, the conversation kept coming back to Pete.

"Tomorrow morning we'll all go meet the first train," proposed Uncle Henry. "And if he isn't on it, then we'll all go find him. Even if it's his own fault, we can't leave him in trouble. Agreed?" The idea cheered up the whole group.

Robert passed around his phony S.D. papers. No one could detect the slightest flaw in them. They were stamped with the seals of the highest German authorities, and one even bore the signature of the head of the S.D. in Amsterdam.

John wanted to tell them what had happened in Amsterdam, but he couldn't bring himself to do it. The free, open atmosphere of former days had not yet returned — maybe because of the anxiety about Pete. Or maybe because there were two newcomers among them. If only Rita had come along! She was still on his mind when he was lying in bed. They had spent two beautiful days together. He had slept in a storage room in the hospital. Had he tried a little harder, he could have persuaded Rita to come back with him. He could tell that she wanted to come. But she had also felt that she couldn't drop her work in Rotterdam unless it was absolutely necessary. She had obligations not only to the hospital but also to all the people she had helped to hide. It was a good thing that he hadn't overdramatized their need. Now they already had two girls in the group.

Sylvia and Angie — he couldn't imagine two girls who were more different. He wondered how they could handle the work. A strange girl — that Sylvia. He couldn't figure her out. Her mind always seemed to be way off somewhere else. Had the interrogations perhaps affected her in some way? That would be tragic; she was such a pretty girl. Maybe the kindness and camaraderie of the group would eventually heal all her internal wounds.

Although Sylvia was very beautiful, he was glad he had an open, sincere girl like Rita. He had promised her that he would see her again soon. No one in Rotterdam knew him, so there was little danger. But if there were danger, would he be able to stay away? He would probably be just as dumb as Pete — if dumb is what that was.

Early the next morning a farm boy of about fifteen came through the front gate, rang the doorbell, and asked for Uncle Henry. He came with news of Pete.

Pete had been visiting his wife and child when the Germans and the Dutch police raided the house one night. He'd tried to escape through the back door, but the house had been surrounded, and they opened fire on him. He was hit twice in the leg, but ran on through hedges and gardens until he reached a haystack, where he passed out. The Germans found him there toward morning when they noticed the farmer's dog barking furiously at the haystack. Apparently the Germans wanted him alive, for they immediately rushed him to the hospital, where Pete had several blood transfusions.

He was now beginning to regain his strength, and he sent them the following message: "I probably won't see you again. I give you all my love. Keep up the good work. Don't try to save me; I'm not worth it."

Joe blew his nose, and Uncle Henry's clenched jaws throbbed with suppressed emotion. The boy looked around the circle of faces and added, "But with such a big group, you men could get him out easy. They put a guard by his bed, but my sister says half the time the man is asleep. And I know a door you can use to sneak into the hospital."

"Your sister? How does your sister know about the guard?" asked Uncle Henry.

"She's Pete's nurse."

"What's your name?"

"Rudy, Sir. Rudy Hoekstra."

Uncle Henry put his hand on the boy's shoulder and said, "Rudy, we appreciate this. You're a brave fellow! We'll go with you right now, if you'll show us the way. Will you do that for us?"

"Great, Sir! Yes, Sir, I sure will!"

Within the hour they were all on a train headed for Pete's hometown. They sat together in the same coach, each with a gun in his pocket.

"If there's a search," Uncle Henry had told them grimly, "we shoot, pull the emergency stop, and make a run for it."

"Oh, nothing will happen," Sylvia said with an indifferent expression. "When you go out looking for danger, that's when it never shows."

And she was right. They made it without incident. At the station, they split into small groups and followed the boy to his home, a small farmhouse on the outskirts of town. There they were received by two nervous but willing parents. Rudy quickly got his bike out and raced to the hospital to summon his sister. When she came in, she brought along the doctor who was treating Pete.

Everybody moved into the living room to discuss plans for Pete's rescue. The Germans had called the hospital earlier that day to ask whether Pete could be moved yet, so the group had to move fast. The doctor couldn't put them off much longer.

"He still needs medical attention," the doctor stressed. "He really ought to be in a hospital for several more days. He has to be handled with care, or his wounds may reopen, and he's still weak from loss of blood."

Uncle Henry knew the director of a T.B. hospital not far from their headquarters. He would be willing to take Pete as a patient. The only problem was how to get him out of the hospital. After an hour of brainstorming, they came up with a plan. The rescue was set for the following evening at five minutes past seven, right after visiting hours started. A little commotion should pass unnoticed then. They would need a car. The car would be parked near the side door, where it would be hidden by shrubbery. While one person stayed with the car, two others would go around the front to keep an eye on the policeman guarding the lobby. The other three would go up to Pete's room dressed in white coats, overpower the guard, and wheel Pete to the side door on a stretcher that would be parked in the hallway outside Pete's room.

However, they would have to get across the Yssel Bridge before the Germans discovered the rescue and got the alarm to the guards on the bridge. The bridge route was risky. But any other route would be much longer and therefore even riskier, so they had to get a fast car. That was going to be the hardest part of the whole adventure. Where were they going to get a car that was still in good shape?

No one had a quick solution, not even the doctor. He, too, drove around in a car with a converter, and his top speed was about 50 kilometres per hour.

"If only you hadn't driven that S.D. car into the drink," Robert said to Sylvia.

"That doesn't help us now," said Uncle Henry. "Anybody got any ideas?"

"I'd be able to get hold of one in my home district," said Joe, "but I couldn't be back by tomorrow evening."

Suddenly John remembered the service station owner at Meppel who had helped Father. Berends was his name. If he remembered right, Berends had once said that he had some cars stashed away to keep them out of German hands. And if Berends didn't have anything, then surely Van der Mey, the policeman, would be able to help them. He had always been generous with his car when an emergency came up.

When John explained why he could be pretty sure of finding a good car by tomorrow afternoon, the spirit of the group quickly revived.

"But I'd like to have someone along who also knows how to drive," said John. "How about you, Joe?"

"Or I could do it," volunteered Sylvia.

"I've got other work in mind for you," Uncle Henry told her. "You're going to go with the doctor, dressed as a nurse, so you can study the layout of the hospital. Make sketches if you get the chance. Miss Hoekstra, can you get word to Pete that help is on the way? Tell him we've decided he's too young to retire. Angie, you're going back home with me. We're going to pick up Leo's S.S. uniform, and we've also got a couple of police uniforms. Remind me to bring the holsters and hats. I'll make sure that they're expecting Pete in the other hospital. Doctor, can you get us some white coats?"

"I've got a couple of extra coats myself," said the doctor. "That ought to be enough. The third man could pretend he's a patient. Miss Hoekstra can get hold of a nurse's uniform for this young lady," he pointed to Sylvia.

"What about me?" asked Rudy. He had been sitting unnoticed in a corner of the room, following the plans intently. He saw himself as a member of the group, and his eagerness to take part in the caper was written all over his face.

"Well, Rudy," said Uncle Henry, smiling affectionately at the boy, "you've already done quite a lot. But if you want to stick with us a little longer, you can be a great help if you show these fellows the way to the hospital and the way from the hospital to the road that goes to the Yssel Bridge. You make sure they know it well, okay? They've got to be able to follow it in their sleep. Right?"

Rudy nodded vigorously and beamed with pride.

Berends, the owner of the service station, was washing up at the pump behind the house when John came walking around the back as Father used to do. The man shook the water out of his eyes and did a double take. "You!" he exclaimed. "I thought you and your dad were in England!"

"What gave you that idea?" asked John, laughing.

"Well, that's the story making the rounds hereabouts, and a while ago I bumped into that old gardener fella of yours — what was his name? — and he sure enough said it was true. You must have been there though, 'cause I heard your name on the radio. For a week straight every night a station in England said, 'John and company have arrived safely.' Wasn't that you? I would have stayed there if I was you."

"No, that wasn't me. It must have been some kind of code," said John. "But that's all right. Keep the story alive. It would be great if everyone here thought we were in England! That would make things a lot safer for us around here."

"I'd still lay low if I were you. I'd sure hate to see them Krauts get their hands on you two. Still in there slugging, are you?"

"That's why I'm here, Mr. Berends. I've got an important errand . . . Say, I've got a friend with me. He's waiting in front of the house. Is it all right if I call him a minute?"

"You should have brought him right with you, man!" said the mechanic. "Any friend of yours is a friend of mine; you should know that."

With his easy laugh and honest face, Joe quickly won the mechanic's trust. They were invited to stay for dinner, but first Berends took them into the living room to talk.

"Okay, let's have it! What do you need?" he said. "Gas, car parts, tires? You underground people are my worst customers. Always want the best and hardly ever pay up. But, okay, I'll survive. Give me the bad news."

He rolled his eyes when he heard that this time they needed a whole car. "Listen, man, I paid out of my own pocket for them cars I got hid away. It's like my life savings, you know . . .! Yes! Well, I guess you'll need something with a little zip for this job. I guess that means the Citroen. You men are really bleeding me, you know that? It's my prize — my pride and joy! And it cost me five thousand guilders."

He paced up and down the room, kicking at the carpet, talking to himself, "But what's a car compared to a man's life, right? I'd turn it over just like that to save you or your father. Good men are hard to come by these days. If I sat on that car now, I'd never get another decent night of sleep. You'll get it, you'll get it! But not a word around my wife. Got that? If she gets wind of it, I still won't get any sleep. I'll be sleeping out in the garage. Okay, but first let's eat."

"Great!" said John happily. "Can I use your phone first? Then I can tell my friends the good news that they can go on with the plans."

He called the doctor they had met at Rudy's house and asked him to tell Uncle Henry that Johnny and Joe had passed their exams.

"Glad to hear it!" he said. "Then Peter should have a chance too. I'll see that they get the good news."

That night John stood at the window in Berends' attic and looked out across the fields. Not many kilometres away lay the ashes of his home, the place where he had spent so many happy evenings with Father and Mother, Fritz, Tricia, Hanneke, Trudy and Hansie. Would they ever have an evening together again?

Suddenly the same strange feeling seized him that had overcome him when he was in the shelter in Grandpa Meyer's house — a moment of inexplicable certainty. He saw the whole family back together in the country. He laughed at his own silly mysticism as he crawled into bed. But he went to sleep with a smile on his face.

It was still dark when Berends shook them awake. After a quick breakfast, he took them to a neighbouring farm. They went into the barn and locked the doors behind them. While the farmer climbed up into the haymow to act as a lookout, Berends and the two boys began digging into the haystack. It was almost noon before they had the car uncovered and ready to drive. They took it for a trial run on a quiet country road behind the farm. The engine hummed like a hummingbird. While the mechanic went home to fetch another can of gas from his garage, John and Joe returned to the barn and put some air in the tires. Berends changed the license plates and pasted a travelling permit on the windshield. They were ready to go!

"We'll bring it back," John promised as they said goodbye. "And if something happens to it, we'll do our best to pay for the damages."

"Sure, and Hitler's my fairy godmother," Berends said gloomily. "Run down a few Germans with it. Then I'll reckon we're even. Be sure to let me know how everything turns out. If anybody tries to flag you down on the way, don't stop. You're sunk driving without papers like you are. Just goose this baby. She'll move out for you! She's a beaut, ain't she?"

Berends walked down the driveway and checked the road. Then he cranked his hand as if to say, "Wind her up!"

"God go with you!" he yelled as they passed him and turned onto the road. He had put his whole gruff soul into those words.

John gave the car a good trial run, and they drove up the Hoekstra driveway a half hour earlier than expected. Rudy stood by the garage door, holding it open.

At six-thirty the group gathered in the living room, checked their guns, and rehearsed the plan down to the smallest detail. Then Uncle Henry led them in prayer.

At ten minutes to seven, John started the car and warmed up the engine. They said goodbye to the Hoekstras, with Rudy standing by looking deeply grieved because he wasn't allowed to go along.

Five minutes to seven.

"Okay, John. Let's go!"

John drove into town, keeping his speed well below the limit. Sylvia, dressed in a nurse's uniform, sat pressed against him. On the other side of her sat Joe, in a police uniform. Robert sat in the back in German uniform, and beside him sat policeman William and Uncle Henry with two white coats in his lap. Angie and Leo had left an hour before to keep an eye on the hospital.

The stillness of early dusk had settled on the streets. No one in the car said anything. The time for talking was past. Never before had they gone into a job under such pressure: this time they were trying to save the life of a friend.

The sidewalk in front of the hospital was busy with people carrying flowers and little parcels. Leo and Angie were standing on the curb.

"All set," said Leo. "Everything's okay. Visiting hours are just starting."

Slowly John followed a gravel drive to the side of the hospital, stopping under a large chestnut tree. Robert and William jumped out and walked toward the front door. Joe stayed with the car. Uncle Henry and Leo put on their white coats, and each took one of John's arms. Sylvia walked ahead of them into the side entrance. Angie came in behind them and stopped at the intersection of two hallways to keep a lookout in two directions.

Not far down the hall stood a guard, rolling a cigarette and eyeing the visitors that came in through the front door. He barely glanced at the group that passed at the end of the hall. Doctors and nurses were constantly going back and forth with patients. His job was to watch the visitors. But then his eyes fell on the flushed young lady standing at the corner. He liked chatting with pretty girls as well as most men.

"Can I help you, Miss? Are you lost?" he asked Angie. "What room are you looking for?"

"Oh, no, thank you. I'm just waiting for my brother. He's undergoing some tests. I'm afraid he's going to need an operation."

"Why don't you come and sit over there in the lobby?" suggested the policeman. "I wouldn't worry too much, if I were you, Miss. Usually you end up worrying for nothing."

"I'm too nervous to sit, thank you. I'd rather wait out here" said Angie, sighing heavily. "What's behind all these doors anyway? They don't look like rooms for patients."

Eager to please, the man pointed out the director's office and the x-ray room, and then began explaining the layout of the whole hospital. Angie secretly motioned Robert back, for he had anxiously approached the front door.

Meanwhile, the others walked up the stairs to the second floor and followed Sylvia down the hall to Pete's room. Rudy's sister met them in the hall and handed Sylvia an overcoat for Pete.

Sylvia strode into the room as if she owned the place. The three men were right on her heels. John took in the situation at a glance. Pete lay in the first of the three beds. He pushed himself up, his face twitching with confused emotions. The policeman sat next to him on a chair. Before he could move, three pistols were aimed at him.

"Hands up, if you please!"

"You here for him?" the policeman asked calmly, raising his hands. "Take him, with my best wishes. I won't give you any trouble."

"Thank you," replied Uncle Henry. "Then you won't mind if I relieve you of this." And he lifted the man's gun from his holster.

"You boys . . ." mumbled Pete emotionally. "You don't know . . . I . . . I . . ."

"Be quiet, and put this on," said Sylvia, handing him the coat.

John helped Pete put on the coat. He heard Uncle Henry order the guard to turn his back, and then he saw the man crumple to the floor as Uncle Henry slugged him with his pistol. They didn't have time to tie and gag the man. When the patient in the bed next to Pete began crying for help, John tried to calm him, but without success. Before John realized what was happening, Sylvia grabbed the water pitcher off the nightstand and knocked the man out cold. Then she brushed the water from her sleeve and didn't waste another glance on her victim.

They didn't need the stretcher. Supported between his two white-clad friends, Pete descended the stairs at a good clip, though he favoured his bad leg. Sylvia took John's arm, and they strolled down the hall, following the others out.

"That was easy," she said, smiling. Was she putting on, or didn't she have a nerve in her body?

Without hesitating or looking up, Uncle Henry and Leo crossed the hall in their white coats, all their attention apparently focused on their patient.

John's glance met Angie's. She was still chatting with the policeman. She laughed at something he said. He heard her say to the policeman, "Excuse me, I've got to go outside a minute. A friend was going to pick us up; I've got to see if he's here yet."

Joe was holding open the car door. Uncle Henry and Leo helped Pete into the back seat. John slid behind the wheel, and Sylvia scooted in next to him. Robert and William came hurrying around the corner and jumped into their seats as the engine purred. Go! There were Leo and Angie strolling down the sidewalk. They would take the train back in the morning. On the other side of the street, someone waved his cap and whistled. Rudy! He had followed them anyway.

"The little rascal," said Uncle Henry, with a chuckle. "Give it the gas, John!"

They went whizzing through streets so dark it was hard to see the intersections. But Robert had memorized the route well.

Behind him William suddenly broke into a song of triumph, "We've got him! We've got him! We have you back, old man, Pete!"

But Pete sobbed. "I'm sorry, Uncle Henry, I just couldn't . . ."

"I know. Relax! It's all over."

"Turn right here," said Robert. "Then we're on the highway. Okay, let's make time, straight ahead!"

"We don't have to worry about anyone behind us," said Sylvia. "All we have to worry about is the telephone."

The tires thrummed on the brick-paved street. John had to concentrate now. The tires squealed as he manoeuvred the car through the curves on the winding road. He kept the speedometer well over a hundred on the straight stretches.

116

"What do you think of the car, Uncle Henry?" asked John.

"Great!" said Uncle Henry. "But will you please try to remember that you've got the best hit squad in the country in the car with you?"

John chuckled. The car responded to his every move. It was a joy to drive! If only they were across that bridge . . .

A small town. Slow down a little. Beside the road stood a policeman. He raised his hand in the Nazi salute as they went whooshing by. Back on the highway, and the gas pedal once again down to the floor. The whine of the tires on the pavement sounded like a song: We've freed our friend; we fear no foe; we're free, we're free!

Now the car was approaching the bridge. They all brought out their guns. "Remember: slow down, but don't stop. Pretend you're going to. But if something goes wrong, floor it. Got that?"

"Yes, Uncle Henry."

Ahead of them a red light moved up and down. The road rose sharply as they neared the bridge. A faint beam of light shone from the doorway of a small guardhouse. In front of it stood two Germans, one with a rifle. They stepped to the edge of the road when the car slowed down. Robert stuck his head out of the window.

"Police!" he shouted in German. "We're in a hurry! Be back in a minute!"

"Drive on," one of the soldiers yelled back, and they were past. That had been easy. Now the guards on the other side. The bridge seemed to go on forever. There it was, like a challenge, the little red light dancing up and down. There were three soldiers this time. Two stepped to the side of the road, but one stayed in the middle with raised arms.

"Run him down," said Sylvia. But John stopped, shifting into first and keeping his foot on the gas. He waited tensely.

"Police, we're in a hurry!" Robert had already hollered in his best German voice. But a flashlight beam shone into the car, and a voice from behind the flashlight demanded, "Travel orders, please!"

"One moment," said Robert, reaching into his coat pocket. The German stepped in front of the car and shone his light on the license plates. Suddenly he straightened up and shouted to the others.

"Go!" shouted Uncle Henry.

The tires squealed. A scream, a loud thump, guns were firing. A bullet screeched by overhead, careening off the roof of the car.

"Faster!" yelled Uncle Henry. But why did he have to poke John so hard as he yelled? He had the gas flat on the floor. The car was nearly flying. The tires hadn't been hit. They had made it!

"Everyone okay? Nobody hit?" Uncle Henry asked anxiously. "You okay, John? You're so quiet."

"Yes, I'm okay," said John. But you didn't have to hit me so hard, he thought to himself. Was that old man powerful!

Watch out! He almost went off the road. All that chatter in the back seat! The fright seemed to have affected him this time. He clenched his jaws as he fought to master himself. He forced back the nausea and shook off the haze that momentarily blinded him. What would the others say if he started vomiting! He would be embarrassed to death in front of Sylvia.

The car hurtled on down the black highway, tires screaming as he swerved around a truck parked on the roadside without any lights. He shot through an S-curve, slowed down for a road sign, and then wheeled the car around a corner onto a secondary road. He felt as if he was driving in a dream, and he trained all his energy on keeping the car on the road.

What a weakling he was! A little excitement, a couple of shots, and he had almost fainted behind the wheel. He was still having trouble controlling the trembling in his arms, and the dizziness kept coming back. He was starting to sweat; he could feel it running down his back. But he wouldn't let it get the best of him. He would force himself! It was just a matter of mind over body. No one need know how hard he was fighting to hold himself together.

"How's it going, John? You haven't said a word," said William, who still knew him the best.

He managed to get out a few words to reassure them — surprisingly chipper. Nobody noticed a thing wrong — not even Sylvia. Especially Sylvia mustn't notice his weakness.

He fought off a powerful impulse to close his eyes and put his head down on the steering wheel. Just to relax — and sleep. He was almost there. He drove through the town, relying completely on the directions being given by Uncle Henry. Then he was steering up the driveway of the other hospital, around the building to the back door where a small, partly screened light burned above a doorway.

"Is this it?" John asked, panting as if he had run a foot race.

"Yes, you can stop here," Uncle Henry's voice said from far, far away. The wheel slipped from his grasp, and the car bumped over the curb into a flower bed.

CHAPTER EIGHT

He didn't want to wake up, but a strange voice kept nagging at him. "Listen. Do you hear me? Yes, open your eyes — all the way. Now look at me. Did you ever have a serum injection before? Do you understand me? A serum injection. Do you know what that is? Have

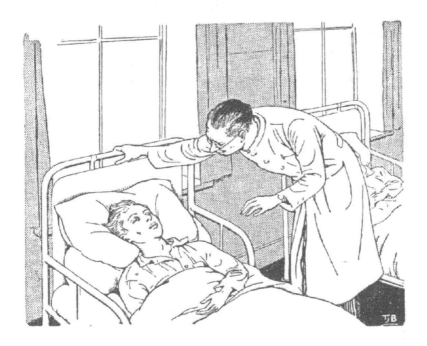

you ever been in a hospital before? Ever been seriously wounded before?"

The man seemed to want him to answer no, and that's how he answered — just to be rid of him. The fellow was a pain in the neck. The loud voice rang in his head.

"Anti-tetanus," he heard the voice say, and then he drifted off again.

When he opened his eyes, he saw Pete lying in a bed next to him, staring at him, his forehead creased with worry. Then Pete held out his hand. John wanted to take it, but he didn't seem to have the strength.

"Where am I?" he whispered, and each word seemed to weigh a ton.

"In the hospital," replied Pete. "But you're not supposed to talk. You've got a bullet in your lung."

Pete was saying something else, but he didn't catch the rest. He lay there grinning to himself.

"Funny," he thought. "A bullet in my lung. How did that get there? Was I born with it?" Then suddenly he saw the red light dancing up and down in front of him, and he felt his fingers tightening on the wheel of a car. A blackness seemed to lift off his mind. He opened his eyes and looked at Pete.

"Then I was . . . I wasn't . . ." he stammered.

"A weakling," he was going to say. "It wasn't fear that made me sick. Ha-ha-ha, I had a bullet in my lung!"

But the room began to lurch, and he closed his eyes. He floated away on a rolling ship into a sunny countryside with green meadows that stretched all the way to an endlessly blue sky.

His secret gladness stayed with him for days — through the attacks of delirium and through the painful treatment of his wound. No pain or misery could rob him of his secret satisfaction. Sometimes he moaned with pain, but whenever he opened his eyes and saw someone at his bed, he managed a smile. As if in a dream, he saw the anxious faces of Uncle Henry and Aunt Nellie, and a kaleidoscope of other familiar faces.

Then, one day, it was Father's face bending over him, and there was fear in his eyes. But there was no fear in John. It never entered his mind that he might die, and he wouldn't have believed it if they had told him so. He was glad — glad and deeply thankful that he hadn't been a coward and that he'd done his job to the end, despite the bullet in his lung.

Not until he was well on the way to recovery did he learn how critically ill he had been. The doctor explained that a rifle bullet had passed through the seat of the car and had entered his chest just under his right shoulder blade. After snapping a rib, it had lodged in the tissue. The bullet itself wasn't so dangerous. It could easily stay there as a souvenir. And the rib would heal soon enough. But when the bullet passed through the seat, it had picked up all kinds of dirt, and an acute infection had spread in his lung. The wound had been cleaned out by a specialist and was still being kept open to allow it to drain. That's why he always had to lie on his left side or on his stomach.

"Understand?" asked the doctor. "To put it in contemporary language: hostile troops suddenly invaded your body; the first attack was repulsed — but only just. The enemy was surrounded by an army of white blood cells, which we are providing with daily enforcements. This good army is slowly but surely destroying the enemy. But it may still take a while before we can announce a complete victory. So here you lie, waging a one-man war!"

John laughed. "I'd rather not serve as a battlefield," he said. "I prefer a battle in which I can do something."

"Well, you can — by taking it easy, resting, and not worrying about anything," said the doctor. "That provides optimum field conditions for victory."

But, like most wars, this one lasted longer than expected. All the leaves had fallen from the birches around the hospital before he was allowed out of bed to take his first steps, holding the arm of a nurse. By that time Pete had long ago vacated the bed next to him. Pete had been laid up for only two weeks, and

122

then he went back to Aunt Nellie's, where he spent a few more weeks convalescing. But now he was doing his share of the work again.

The group didn't forget John. When he was finally allowed to have regular visits, someone showed up almost every day to give him a running account of their doings. They had finally pulled off the town hall caper that they had planned so long. They stole the records of the population of an entire district and burned them. Without these records, the Germans would have a harder time tracing people. Nor would the Nazis know what families had young men of working age for the German factories.

Their holdup of a second distribution centre netted nearly 12,000 ration cards. Another time they got wind of a black marketeer who was selling bicycle tires for 100 guilders apiece. One night they "bought out" his entire stock, leaving behind ration cards and the established market price of the tires. The tires were passed on for use by underground workers.

One day when Sylvia was visiting him, Rita came walking in. John introduced the two girls to each other, and they sat on opposite sides of the bed sizing each other up, Rita surreptitiously, but Sylvia brazenly, almost insolently. John tried to keep the conversation going, but after a while he gave up. Rita sat stiffly in her chair and acted very cold. John thought she was jealous, and Sylvia seemed to think the same thing, for a scornful smile glimmered in her eyes and turned up the corners of her mouth as she said goodbye.

"You live in Rotterdam?" she asked Rita.

"Yes."

"You're a nurse, you say?"

"I was."

"Whereabouts do you live?"

Then Rita gave her a wrong address.

John was about to ask: Have you moved? Why aren't you at the hospital anymore? But a look from Rita kept him still.

"John," she asked, annoyed, when the door had closed behind Sylvia, "what kind of woman is that?"

"She's our courier," explained John. "What's the matter, don't you like her?"

"I should say not!" said Rita vehemently. "I can't stand that type of person. What business is it of hers where I live? You don't ask questions like that nowadays. John, don't you dare tell her anything about me. I mean it!"

"She's got a lot of courage," John countered, "and she's proved herself completely trustworthy. I could tell you stories about her that would . . ."

"Do you think she's beautiful?" asked Rita.

John laughed. So she *was* jealous after all.

"Yes, I think she's very beautiful," he said, "but I don't think she's very lovable, like you. Come here a minute before the nurse comes back."

Two days later, he had the surprise of his life. He was sitting in the sun porch on a lounge chair with some tubercular patients — this was actually a T.B. hospital — when they came walking toward him, bright in the winter sun: Father and Mother, walking arm in arm. Suddenly he was back in prewar days; this was how he had often seen them come strolling through the garden. They hadn't seen him among all the other patients, and he had momentarily lost his voice and power of movement.

But when they turned to go to the door, John suddenly threw off his blanket and hurried to intercept them. It was against the doctor's orders, and the nurse came running after him, but he went on. He wanted to reassure Mother by showing her how well he was doing. As punishment he was immediately returned to his bed, but by then they were already together, seeing and touching one another.

"You have it made here," Father said approvingly. "Don't be in a hurry to get out. Make sure that you've completely recuperated first."

John knew what Father was thinking. As long as he was here, he was safe. Now that he was on the way to recovery, Father was almost thankful for the bullet that had wounded him. But Father himself was still busy. After half an hour he looked at his watch and explained that he had an appointment he couldn't skip. Even for today he had been unable to free himself entirely.

But the next day he and Mother were back again. Uncle Henry had found them a place to stay not far from the hospital, and they stayed for almost a week. They talked about things that had been on their minds for so long, things they had been unable to share with each other.

After Father had left, Mother came a final time by herself. Then John told her about the dreams that he had had, first in Amsterdam and then at Berends' house. But he didn't tell her about being trapped in a shelter, almost despairing of life. Father had said nothing of that experience either. "All of us were walking through the garden together, just as we used to," John said, describing his dream. "And it was as if a voice was telling me that one day we would be together again just as we were before. Who knows, Mom, maybe it will come true in a couple of months. Even the Nazis are starting to talk about the invasion. It can't be much longer."

"I hope you're right," said Mother, with a sigh. "Our house is gone, and our money is *almost* gone, but as long as we all make it to the end, I don't care if everything else is gone. As long as we have each other!"

A few days later, Angie came in to see John, full of anxiety. She had just gone to Amsterdam with Sylvia to deliver several packages of ration cards. As they were packing them, she had noticed Sylvia putting a bundle into her purse, but she had thought nothing of it at the time.

She and Sylvia had agreed to rendezvous where the Keizer and Spiegel canals met. Angie arrived first, but because it was drizzling, she sought shelter in a portico. Sylvia came back with a strange man, a shady-looking character in a leather cap and coat, and she saw Sylvia giving the man the ration cards in exchange for a handful of bills.

Now Angie knew why Sylvia always seemed to have plenty of money to buy expensive clothes on the black market. No, she hadn't talked about it with Sylvia. She was afraid of her. But she couldn't very well just let her get away with it, could she?

"Do you think I should just forget about it?" she asked John.

"No, I certainly don't," he said, troubled. He could hardly believe it! Was this the secret behind those beautiful eyes? Such a mean, grubby little secret?

"Tell Uncle Henry," he told her. "Or wait, maybe you shouldn't just yet. You really ought to confront her first, Angie. Maybe she needed money real bad! You know, family problems or something. Or maybe that man she met knows something about her and he's blackmailing her. Sure, such things *do* happen. It's probably something like that. I thought that she had a mother to support. Didn't Robert say something like that once?"

"I don't know," said Angie. "That's the way it is. She knows everything about us, but we don't know a thing about her. No, I'm not going to talk to anybody else about it! Uncle Henry won't believe me. And if I say anything that gets around, Robert will never speak to me again. He's crazy about her!"

Finally they agreed that John would speak to Sylvia. If she could explain what she had done and if she promised that it would never happen again, they would leave it at that. Otherwise they would have to go to Uncle Henry.

"Better send her here as soon as possible," suggested John. "The sooner this is over and done with, the better."

"How do I do that?" asked Angie. "She'll suspect something right away. She's as cunning as a . . . as a fox! But maybe I can think of some errand."

First Rita, and now Angie. Other women seemed to distrust Sylvia instinctively. Was it partly jealousy?

When Sylvia finally showed up after two days, she was with Uncle Henry. They came to say that Joe had been killed. They had been robbing another distribution centre, and Joe had been on lookout at the front door when the National Guard, the N.S.M. police force, had suddenly showed up. Joe had immediately sounded a warning and then had covered the squad's retreat. But he had been killed in the gun battle.

John was deeply stricken. Why Joe? Of the whole group, he had been the most hopeful, the strongest. Why did the man who seemed to love life the most have to die first?

He was glad that Uncle Henry and Sylvia didn't stay long. He lay down and sobbed into his pillow. But when he calmed down, the thought came to him that Joe had died for a handful of ration cards — the same cards that Sylvia had traded on the black market for pretty clothes.

He walked to a doctor's office, picked up a phone, and called Aunt Nellie's. Angie answered; he told her to send Sylvia back to see him as quickly as possible. He no longer cared whether she suspected something.

She came the next morning. He was not surprised at her response to his challenge.

"I don't have to answer you; I don't have to tell you anything," she replied venomously. "But I'll say this much. It's all a lie! I've got sources of income that you and Angie know nothing about. And it's none of your business. It's personal! And I'm warning you, don't you dare repeat those lies!"

As she hissed her warning, she rose and stepped toward the door. Before he could respond, the door slammed behind her. "Now what?" he wondered. Her warning had sounded like a threat. But the worst she could do was leave the group and join another one, wasn't it? The rest of the group wouldn't like that at all, especially not Uncle Henry; she was irreplaceable. But shouldn't Uncle Henry know about this?

He didn't get long to think it over, however. Everything seemed to be going wrong at once. That afternoon he was called to the director's office, where he found Dick Vriend sitting, looking intense and sad. He knew at once that something had happened to Father. He was surprised at his own calm as he heard Vriend tell him that Father had been arrested. It was almost as if he had always known that this would happen.

Vriend tried to soften the shock by saying that Father's situation didn't look too bad. But John didn't believe him. Hope seemed to have drained out of him in one swift rush.

"He was stopped in an ordinary street check," Vriend told him, "and nothing would have happened if he hadn't been carrying a package of I.D. seals in his briefcase. You know what I.D. seals are, don't you? Or have you been out too long?

"Pretty soon now, every person in the country will be ordered to report to their local town hall to show their I.D. and registration card. Everyone will be issued a new registration card and get a little seal stuck on their I.D. Without both, you can't get ration cards. If we aren't prepared, it will be disastrous for all divers and fugitives. Without the seals, their I.D.'s will be useless. They'll be spotted instantly at any check. So we're printing seals or stealing them and then distributing them to all the divers."

"And you don't think it's dangerous to be caught with a package of seals in your briefcase?" John asked bitterly.

"Listen a minute! The paper that the seals were wrapped in was filthy. You know how hard it is to get your hands on a decent piece of wrapping paper. So your father told them that he had just found it on the street and was on his way to the police station when he was stopped and searched. They must have put some stock in his story, because he was put in a cell with three other men who were there for minor offenses. He hasn't been subjected to interrogation yet. But, sure, there's always the chance that the Germans will find out who he really is. They don't let people go very readily these days."

"So? That gives you reason to be optimistic?"

"Now wait! I'm not finished," said Vriend. "We've established regular contact with him through an S.S. guard whom we bribe to smuggle in notes. Your father hasn't given up hope — he especially told me to tell you that. One of these days we're going to make an attempt to get him out. We're working on a high-ranking S.D. officer who, I think, we can bribe or blackmail into helping us. We've collected 20,000 guilders to buy your father's freedom. So there's still lots of hope, John. He'll probably be back with us in a couple of days. In fact, I'm almost sure of it! I'll call you as soon as he's safe and sound."

John waited for three days. Then he couldn't stand it anymore. He talked to his doctor, who was reluctant to let him go because he hadn't yet recovered his full strength. But in the end the doctor lent him a warm overcoat, and an hour later John was sitting in the train. Soon he was in Amsterdam, looking up Vriend. That night they got the news.

They had failed, and failed miserably. The attempt to ransom Father had backfired. From the high sum that had been offered for Father's freedom, the Germans had concluded that he must be someone important. So they had transferred him from the local prison to a maximum security prison, where he had been subjected to intense interrogation.

John stayed in Amsterdam. Day after day he was out with Dick Vriend looking for a guard at the new prison who would be willing to contact Father. They finally found a man, a captain of the guards, who had cooperated with the underground on other occasions. When he met them the following day, however, he told them that there was nothing he could do. Father had been put in a part of the prison that was very closely guarded by German soldiers. That was all he could find out.

John couldn't decide what to do next. Walking by himself, he roamed through the city, and after a while he found himself near the prison. Walking along the canal, he looked across the water at the massive prison walls and the small, barred windows. Then he tore himself away, knowing that if he kept looking, his self-control would fail him.

What Uncle Henry had said after Joe's death was true: You had to discipline yourself to be hard and to think of your duty. Carry on, with a wounded heart and gritted teeth. You were in a war! At stake was not the happiness of the individual, but the victory and freedom of the people.

He returned to Vriend's house to say goodbye, and he caught a train up north, to Mother. She was still living in excruciating uncertainty, for she hadn't received any news of Father for two full weeks. Now it was especially important for John to be strong so that he could comfort her.

In the train he thought of what he might say. He framed brave, noble sentences in his mind, a passage from Scripture, a word of encouragement from a speech by the Queen.

But when he found her that night in the bare kitchen of an abandoned farmhouse and saw the helpless sorrow in her eyes, when he realized how empty life would be for her if Father did not come back, his strength suddenly gave out. He sobbed out their mutual grief with his head in her lap.

CHAPTER NINE

During the next few months, the war between the resistance and the Nazis intensified.

On New Year's Eve, John brought Mother and the two youngest children, Hansie and Trudy, to friends in Groningen, the northernmost province. Here she would have someone to look out for her, and she would have more to occupy her mind than in that lonely farmhouse. He stayed in town overnight.

In the middle of the night, he heard shooting in the street. The next morning he learned that several prominent citizens known to be anti-German had been hauled out of bed and shot down in front of their homes. The Germans called it "taking reprisals." Apparently a policeman who had been cooperating with the S.D. had been executed the day before by a resistance group. By giving it the name of "reprisal," the Nazis tried to legitimize their reign of terror.

About two weeks later, while John was visiting Uncle Gerrit in his little house along the canal, the Hoving farm was raided during the night by the Dutch Nazi organization called the National Guard, reinforced by German soldiers. After a short struggle, the farmer and his son were overpowered and taken to the camp at Westerbork, where they were executed the following day.

The four Jews hiding on the Hoving farm were also sent to Westerbork and relayed to a German death camp on the first available transport.

They included the parents of Marie, the little girl who had been part of John's family for a long time and who was now living with the Biemolts. Marie would not find out about her parents' fate until the end of the war.

Mrs. Hoving and her daughter were driven from their house. Furniture, tools, supplies, and farm animals were carried off by the Nazis. People watched in shock from behind their curtains, and those who were hiding divers asked themselves when their turn would come. But the cruelty and terror softened no one's resistance. Instead, hatred for those who collaborated with the enemy intensified.

Two days later, one of the National Guard who had participated in the raid on the Hoving farm suddenly disappeared without a trace. A boatman found him floating in the canal and told Uncle Gerrit. He told the boatman to keep quiet about it, and he and John tied sandbags to the body so that it wouldn't be found again. An N.S.M. farmhand moved into the empty Hoving house and tried to ingratiate himself with his neighbours, but no one would have anything to do with him. He and his family lived off the supplies that had been left behind.

The National Guard was a great danger to John as he visited in his home district, for the local N.S.M. farmers knew John. Now they were patrolling the roads every day with hunting rifles. Even at night John had to be careful. When he was out on his bicycle, he sped away from anyone riding behind him, and whenever he came into a room, he positioned himself so that he could keep an eye on the door and windows.

As he stayed on with Uncle Gerrit, he was quickly regaining his health and strength. The old man credited it to country air and the farm diet.

Uncle Gerrit's age was starting to catch up with him. Some mornings he was bent over with rheumatism. But he faithfully took care of the old place, tending the orchard and the bees. He had saved the proceeds from fruit and honey to help rebuild the house.

The bricks of the old house were neatly stacked in the yard, the mortar having been chipped off carefully. Uncle Gerrit had cleared away the ashes and other rubble, and as soon as the frost was out of the ground, he planned to start digging the new foundations. He was still the same old optimist. They would be able to start building this coming summer, he assured John, as if Churchill had given him a personal guarantee that the invasion would come this spring.

Even the N.S.M. leader, Mussert, had referred to the impending invasion in his New Year's speech, and the Nazi papers regularly printed directions on how the people were to conduct themselves in the event of an Allied invasion.

Despite the increasing tension, old Uncle Gerrit still hadn't lost his sense of humour. And he wasn't worried at all about Father — if you believed him. Dick Vriend had told them that Father had been transported to Germany, apparently to Dachau. When Uncle Gerrit heard the news, his face brightened as if it were a good report.

"They didn't line him up against the wall, did they? And he's still alive," said Uncle Gerrit. "Now I'm sure he'll make it to the end of the war!"

"How can you say that, knowing what it's like in those camps?" exclaimed John despairingly.

"Sure, it's bad," replied Uncle Gerrit. "But your father's got something, a spark that they're not going to snuff out so easily. I've known your father since he was a little lad, and I'm telling you, if anyone can survive, he can. Just think of Mr. Wiesel. Your father is just as tough as he is. Fritz can tell you about him. He spent almost a year in the camp at Vught. Sure, it was a terrible ordeal! He came out nothing but skin and bones. But he's back to his old self again. And your father won't have to wait a year till he's freed.

Just wait and see! And when he gets home, we'll fix him up as good as new. With your mom's cooking . . . Oh boy, I tell you, it'll be no time at all . . . no time at all."

Tricia and Fritz were present when the old man was saying this, and Tricia brightened up noticeably. So John didn't say anything. Tricia was facing her final exams, as John had last year. She was staying with a teacher and working hard. Sundays she spent with Mother.

Fritz's last report was very poor. He couldn't study, he said. What did he care about all those silly books when the family was all broken up and the rest of life was coming apart at the seams, too? Maybe when — or if — things got back to normal, he'd think about school again. He could recite all the goings-on in the district, however, and he could describe in detail the latest developments on all the battlefronts. He was supposed to be working for room and board with a baker who had befriended him, but he showed up there only at night to eat and sleep.

He was willing to do anything for Mr. Wiesel, his old teacher, and he came knocking at his door regularly, carrying baskets of food that he had scrounged up no one knew where. A week after he arrived home from the concentration camp, Mr. Wiesel returned to school, leaning on a cane. He had been strictly forbidden to talk about the camp, but if anyone wanted to know about the camps, said Mr. Wiesel, they had only to look at him.

The other teacher, Mr. Van der Broek, whom Fritz had once held in such high esteem for his classroom statements against the Nazis — but who had been afraid to hide a Jewish girl — had also been imprisoned. But just for saying OSO once too often, Fritz said. They put him in a cell overnight.

One policeman said that he had wailed and sobbed so loudly all night long that the Germans had turned him loose the next morning to be rid of the noise. But now he swaggered about town as if he had endured all that the enemy could dish out. "And then I have to sit in class listening to a creep like that!" snorted Fritz. "No thanks!" He cut all of Van der Broek's classes, and the principal turned a blind eye.

"There's more important stuff to do," Fritz said.

"Like what?" his brother asked.

Fritz caught himself. "I promised not to tell anyone."

"Now, listen here, Fritz, you're too young for this sort of work," said John, worriedly. "I wish you'd drop it!"

"Too young?" Fritz asked. "How old were *you* when the war started and you went out with Father and Uncle Gerrit to fish guns out of the canal? Think back! Just as old as I am now."

"But it's a lot more dangerous now!" argued John. "The Germans are much more vicious, and they're smarter."

"So are we," replied Fritz. "We're not as dumb as you used to be — to go out unarmed or to hold a secret meeting with a Nazi next door watching everything."

"Dad wouldn't like it," John said as a last resort.

"Yes, let's talk about Dad," Fritz said sharply. "While Dad's being starved and worked to death in Dachau, I'm supposed to sit around here and play the fair-haired little boy — is that what you want? Let me tell you this, John: if Dad dies in that camp, I'm going to sink half a dozen of those devils in the canal! See if I don't!"

"Sixteen," John said, as if to himself.

"Yes, sixteen!" repeated Fritz. "Almost seventeen, in fact. Have you seen the latest occupation troops the Germans are sending? The older ones are all going to the Eastern front. Some of the ones coming in are no older than I am. But they do just as good a job as those slow old men."

"Hey, easy on the oldies! Show a little respect!" said Uncle Gerrit. But no one laughed.

John didn't press it. He didn't have the heart to bump heads with his brother. In his mind, he saw Fritz dangling on the cable of the runaway balloon and heard Uncle Gerrit saying, "Once he latches onto something, he sure doesn't let go." He was tempted to close his eyes and let come what may. The daily struggle and misery exhausted him; he was sick and tired of it. He just didn't have the energy to take on anything more. Maybe he hadn't yet recovered completely from his wound.

A strange listlessness also kept him from the group. He could have been helping out by now. Two letters had reached him from his comrades, passed along by Van der Mey. Things were going well, and they were keeping busy, said the letters. Besides some smaller jobs, they had pulled a raid on a district labour office and destroyed all their records. It would be a long time before any more young men would be called up in that district for service in Germany. Now they were planning another distribution office robbery.

After Joe's death, two more young men had joined the group. But John's place remained open, wrote Uncle Henry; they all missed him. The second letter had been signed by each member of the group.

"My heart pines for you," Sylvia had written in a fancy, flowing script with curls and scrolls that covered half the page. They were the words of a popular American song she liked to sing. That's how she was. Feelings were a joke. But apparently she had forgotten her anger just before John had left the hospital. Sometimes he even missed her.

After reading the letter, he decided that he was honour-bound to return to the group and get back into the struggle. He decided to leave the next morning. But when he searched his wallet for a train schedule that he had put there, he came across a faded photograph of Father. He once more heard him saying, with an edge of desperation in his voice, "One of us has to survive, John!" When he remembered that night of hiding and near suffocation, his courage almost failed him.

Again, it was William who roused him from his indecision. One foggy day in February, he suddenly came barging into the little house along the canal, looking as wild-eyed and shaky as the first time John had seen him. With rage and despair, he told John that the group had been wiped out. Uncle Henry and Pete had been killed. The two new members, Louis and Ted, had been taken prisoner, and so had Angie and Aunt Nellie. Sylvia had done it — betrayed them all! That cold, insidious snake! That heartless witch with the beautiful mask! That she-devil! William couldn't find words enough to express his hate and grief.

It had all happened only yesterday. Everyone had been home except Robert, who'd gone to Utrecht for a meeting. Sylvia and Angie were off in another room by themselves, and suddenly there was screaming and shouting. Sylvia had struck Angie, and then Angie started shouting accusations which had dumbfounded the rest of them. Apparently Sylvia had secretly sold over 200 ration cards on the black market. Uncle Henry had taken charge and questioned both girls. Sylvia's guilt had been proven beyond any doubt.

Uncle Henry was furious. The young woman had just stood there, though, looking at them with that cold, scornful smirk. Finally he had ordered her to go upstairs and stay there until Robert returned. Then she would hear her sentence. Perhaps the word sentence was the cause of the betrayal.

When Robert got home at about ten o'clock, he refused to believe a word of Angie's story, and got into a loud argument with Uncle Henry. He went running up to Sylvia's room and found it empty. Immediately he put his coat back on and went to search for her in town.

"If she doesn't come back," he had shouted at Uncle Henry, "I'm not coming back either." Then he slammed the door and left.

"Leo and I went after him to calm him down," William went on, "and that's what saved us. We went with him to check several places where Sylvia might have gone, and at the last address, since it was already past curfew, we decided that she had probably returned home. We talked Robert into taking a calm look at things and then we went sneaking back home about twelve-thirty. When we got there, the police van was already in front of the house. She must have gone straight to the S.D.

"Not that we suspected her right away. But at the station one of the Germans let her name slip, and a loyal police officer who was at the booking heard it. Later he also managed to talk to Aunt Nellie. She said that the S.D. had suddenly been inside the house, without any kind of warning. Even the dog hadn't barked.

"Remember how when some of us were still out after curfew Aunt Nellie used to hide the key outside? Well, the Germans must have known exactly where to find it. Maybe she was even with them and let them in. Louis and Ted were arrested in their beds,

139

but Uncle Henry and Pete, who were sleeping in another room, put up a fight and were both killed. When the house was searched, the S.D. knew exactly where to look. One of them went straight to the chair that had all our guns inside it. They got everything! Nothing's left, John!

"They even got the car. That witch had picked it up at nine o'clock. We kept the car hidden at the mortuary, with the hearse. The groundskeeper didn't suspect anything was wrong, of course, because she was always the one who came to pick up the car and drop it off. Is that why she did it, John? So she could ride around like a fancy lady? Did she betray us all for a handful of ration cards? It seems unbelievable — Uncle Henry and Pete . . . unbelievable . . ."

He lapsed into silence and sat quivering, his face in his hands. Uncle Gerrit got up, took a bottle from the cupboard and poured something into a glass.

"Here, drink that down. It'll help calm your nerves," he said, but William didn't seem to hear.

"We were just a bunch of innocent little boys," he said as if dazed. "Infatuated! We were no match for her. Robert should have seen through her. But, no, he was blinder than any of us. I think he was in love with her."

Guilt rose in John's throat like bile. He, too, should have seen through her two months ago in the hospital.

"I'm warning you . . ." she had said. Now he knew what that warning had meant. The secret behind those beautiful eyes had been raw self-interest. When she found her ambitions blocked, she cold-bloodedly destroyed them all. Or had she been in cahoots with the S.D. from the beginning? But he — John De Boer — had crawled into his shell in fear of those withering eyes. He had failed to warn Uncle Henry; he had put the whole matter out of his mind.

"Oh, God, what are we going to do now?" John asked, as a prayer of desperation.

"You've got to help me save whoever we can," said William. "That's why I'm here. The witch knows Van der Mey's address, so he has to be warned. The last letter you got, she mailed! Don't think she's forgotten you either. But Uncle Gerrit can warn him. We've got to go to Amsterdam right now. You know some of the places where Uncle Henry used to go. I don't. Take along as much money as you can; I'm nearly broke.

"That woman's holding all the cards, man. She went *everywhere* with Uncle Henry. We warned as many people in town and in the area as we could last night, and this morning Leo and I called up whoever we could get hold of. Robert gave us some addresses, but for the rest he's useless. He hasn't exactly gone crazy, but he's obsessed with only one thought — to find her. He has a pretty good chance, too. He knows all her friends in Rotterdam and Leiden, and he can go where he wants with his S.D. papers. I hope he finds her quick!

"If she starts testifying against the other fellows and against Aunt Nellie and Angie, they're dead. She knows everything about them. Maybe we can still help them. I've agreed to meet Robert at a certain spot tomorrow night. There are still four of us. She hasn't destroyed us all yet! But I don't even have a gun anymore."

"I can help you there, my boy," Uncle Gerrit broke in. "I've got a dilly of a pistol hidden in one of my beehives. That one, third from the left! There should be some bullets there too, wrapped in a rag. Well, I'd better get going to warn Van der Mey."

Grunting, he pulled on a wool jacket and then walked back to the table, his toothless mouth like a grim wound in his dark, wrinkled face.

"I've never prayed for anyone's death before," he said. "This is the first time!"

They didn't make it to Amsterdam that night. On the other side of Meppel, their train was strafed by English fighters. The engine came to a halt, clouds of steam billowing out through several large holes. The passengers fled screaming into the ditches. Several people in the first car had been hit.

But William and John didn't have time to help. They cut across the fields to a highway and thumbed a ride on a truck. The man took them to Zwolle where they warned one of Uncle Henry's contacts. They stayed overnight at the trucker's house and persuaded him to take them to Amersfoort. They would leave at four o'clock the next morning. It cost them William's gold ring, John's watch, and fifty guilders. But they were past caring. Time was far more important than money.

They lay tossing and turning for a couple of hours in the frigid little attic room. John's thoughts kept returning to Uncle Henry and the others, but he couldn't let himself think only of that. What was the name of the radio man in Utrecht who sometimes did business with Uncle Henry? Would he be able to find the house in the south end of Amsterdam where the first meeting had been held with Father and the other L.O. men? Uncle Henry had gone there several times afterwards, taking Sylvia along to carry papers. No, he shouldn't start thinking of Uncle Henry again! This was no time for grieving. He must not allow his mind to be distracted by memories. He *had* to go on! He had to concentrate on present dangers, to save whatever lives he could!

They chugged into Amersfoort at dawn. The trucker tried to squeeze an extra ten guilders out of them, but William suddenly lost his temper and told him that he might get a punch in the mouth but he

142

wasn't going to get another penny out of them. The two friends split up at the railway station, William heading for Utrecht and then The Hague, and John for Amsterdam.

Less than two hours later, John was at Dick Vriend's house. He gave John the address in the south end and a couple of other addresses where Uncle Henry might have been with Sylvia. He also told John that Grandpa Meyer and Mrs. Steen had both died in prison and that Sophie was in the camp at Vught. But John was no longer moved. He couldn't afford to be.

He went to the address in the south end of the city, and there he was given another address. The woman recognized him and invited him in for a cup of coffee, but he turned her down. She should get out as soon as possible, he stressed. He hit all the other addresses with his terrible warning and then stopped at a vegetable stand and bought a big carrot, for he didn't have a single ration card. He had to pay an exorbitant price for the half-frozen carrot.

As he walked down the street munching on it, he thought of professor Van Loon who had once obtained information about Father for him. Van Loon had also known Uncle Henry. John arrived at the house sooner than he had expected, and he stood on the sidewalk for a minute finishing his carrot. As he stepped to the door to ring the bell, he was suddenly seized by such a fearful premonition that he quickly turned and walked on. He tried to force himself to go back. This was silly! Then he remembered that Van Loon had a telephone. So he dialed Van Loon's number from a nearby café.

"Ja, hallo," said a voice, "dis is Von Loon."

John hung up without answering. The Germans had beaten him there and had already staked out the house.

His mind hardly even registered how miraculously he had been saved, for in the café an old record player began piping out a familiar tune: "My heart pines for you," the words Sylvia had written behind her name. For the first time he "pined" for her too. Hatred stirred in his heart. He hurried to the railway station to catch the train to Leiden.

That evening the four remaining members of the group sat together in a barren, rented room and decided that Leo and William would go to Utrecht where Aunt Nellie and the others were imprisoned to see whether anything could be done to help them. John and Robert, meanwhile, would go back to Amsterdam because Robert was convinced that they had a good chance of finding Sylvia there. He had discovered that she was hooked up with an S.D. officer who was stationed in Amsterdam.

The night she had betrayed them, she made a call to Amsterdam, and the S.D. in Utrecht had received its instructions from there. Robert didn't say how he had come by this information; in fact, he didn't say any more than was absolutely necessary, and he didn't mention Sylvia's name. In his eyes there was a detached, faraway look.

For three days they searched without any leads. Then, one afternoon, John was walking along the main street in one of the suburbs of Amsterdam when he suddenly heard the familiar sound of the Citroen behind him.

"It's her!" he thought. "Don't turn your head!" But he couldn't resist. There was Sylvia behind the wheel of the Citroen, wearing a silver-gray fur coat and smoking a cigarette. Beside her sat a man in civilian clothes. She took her cigarette from her mouth and laughed at something the man had said. John felt her glance passing over him, and then she was past. The Citroen shifted into high gear and sped off

toward the centre of the city. She hadn't noticed him!
Or had she? He still seemed to feel her eyes on him.

He was running now, hugging the buildings. If
he could reach the corner in time, he would be able
to see which way she turned.

But when he arrived at the corner, the asphalt road
lay quiet and deserted, shrouded in long shadows.
How would he track her down now? He followed the
road to where it ran dead into a park. She would have
had to turn either toward the city centre or away from
it. He began walking toward the city — not that he
had any hope of tracing her now. Coming to a small
square, he suddenly stopped, his heart pounding vio-
lently. There, under the trees, stood the black Citroen.
Despite its German military plates, John would have
recognized Berends' car anywhere.

He ran down the street looking for a place to call
from, praying that Robert would be home. It wasn't
very likely. But when he called, Robert answered the
phone himself. A few words were sufficient. Less than
ten minutes later, they were walking toward each

other about a block from where John had found the car.

The car was still there. Dusk was settling on the city. Music carried outdoors from a couple of expensive bars nearby.

They had plenty of time now. But they were both breathing hard. Nevertheless, Robert's voice was calm and alert.

"Say what you will," he said, "you've got to admit that I have more right to her than you. Besides, I've got the gun. You do whatever you like; I'm staying with the car. Maybe I'll crawl into the back seat. Sooner or later she'll be back here."

Even though he wasn't armed, John felt that he had to stay. He circled the square, slowly approaching one of the bars. Maybe he could find out where she was. "My heart pines for you . . ." A doorman, his gold braid glittering in the last rays of the setting sun, buttonholed him and invited him in. He began to turn away, but then stopped and asked the man if he had seen a lady in a gray fur coat go inside.

After the words were out, he caught himself. "That was foolish!" he thought. He ignored the man's offer to escort him inside so that he could take a look around, and he began moving away when he sensed someone behind him. Something hard poked into his back. A voice rasped behind him, "If you turn around, you're dead! You're under arrest." Someone grabbed his arm and then his other arm, and his hands were cuffed behind him.

CHAPTER TEN

After the first shock, he felt remarkably light-headed — almost relieved. Finally it had happened. What he had feared for many months was now a reality. Now there was no more reason to fear it.

He was hustled along past the dark houses and store fronts. The thought flashed through his mind that Robert might help him. But, no, Robert had to get *her.* He resisted the temptation to look in the direction of the car. Robert must not fail. He himself was out of it now. Sylvia must have recognized him after all and set up this trap for him. Now maybe she would be off her guard. She would go to the car thinking that the coast was clear. She might be holding all the cards as William had said, but now she had been trumped.

Would he be linked to her death? What did they have on him? He had nothing in his possession but his I.D., which was completely in order. There was no law against stopping at a bar.

He straightened up and looked at the two men who were pulling him along. The soldier holding him by the handcuffs was considerably shorter than he was; the other one, the man with the raspy voice, held him lightly by one arm. The smell of perfume clung to his suit. If only he weren't cuffed . . .

They reached the corner. Ahead was the canal. A girl stopped on the sidewalk and watched him being hustled off. He couldn't see her face in the dark, but she reminded him of Tricia.

The short one yanked the cuffs so that they cut his wrists.

"What do you want from me?" asked John.

"Be quiet!" growled the other and kicked John in the leg.

Around another corner. Down a narrow passage between two buildings, their footsteps echoing hollowly. A peeling door. The small one rang a bell. A heavy man in a black uniform opened the door. A musty, shadowed hallway. Down the hall to a steel gate that reached from floor to ceiling. The key grated in the lock, and the gate clanged shut behind them. Keys rattled, and John began to feel the panic of a caged animal. Had Father, too, passed down this hall two months ago? The thought gave him a strange sense of satisfaction.

In a bare room lit by bright lights, his handcuffs were removed. He rubbed his wrists. Another official in a black uniform, older than the one who had let them in, was standing behind a table. The raspy-voiced German suddenly grabbed John by the front of his shirt and slammed him against the wall. For the first time, he got a good look at the man's face. He was the man who had been in the car with Sylvia.

"Now, what was it you wanted? Does this make you happy, eh?" With each question, he smacked John against the wall. John trembled with anger and struggled to keep his self-control. It would be foolish to strike back here!

"No answers?" Another bump.

"I don't know what you're talking about!" he said, and he was disgusted at the quaver in his voice. "Wasn't I supposed to be standing there?"

"He doesn't know!" Thump! "Then why were you asking about a lady in a fur coat?" Thump! "What did you want with her?" Thump!

"Oh that? I was just looking for my sister." He was startled to hear the lie coming from his mouth. He had spoken before he had even thought up the story. "I asked the doorman . . ."

"Your sister, eh?" Thump! The man released his shirt. "So the lady in the fur coat is your sister? Well, in a few minutes you'll be reunited with your sister. Won't that be wonderful? We'll see how your sister welcomes you."

Not if Robert has anything to say about it, thought John.

"Lock him up," said the man. "We'll be back shortly!"

The official saluted. The Germans started to go. He had to play his part to the hilt.

"Just a minute! You can't do this! You can't just lock up somebody who hasn't done anything!"

The taller man came back.

"Who do you think you are, telling us what we can and can't do?"

His face was only inches from John's. And then John went crashing back into the wall once more, tasting the blood in his mouth. He still felt the man's knuckles on his jaw. The two men went out the door laughing loudly.

"I wouldn't look at them like that, if I were you," cautioned the old official. "That will only get you more beatings. Come over here and empty your pockets. You from out of town?"

With a shaking hand, John pulled out his wallet, a pocketknife, and his I.D., and put them on the table in front of the old man. His handkerchief was given back.

The old man studied his I.D. and then went through his wallet. A sheaf of papers and photos slid out on the table. John got a sudden scare, for among the papers was another I.D. He had two I.D.'s identical except for the place of residence. One said Meppel, and the other Amsterdam. He used the one with the Meppel address when he was visiting his home province; residents from the big cities raised suspicion. The old man's bushy eyebrows hid his eyes as he bent over the papers. He looked at the second I.D. and asked John, "Where did you say you were from?"

"Meppel."

"Are you sure?"

"Yes, Sir."

One I.D. went back into the wallet. The other had disappeared. He knew better than to say thank you. The man looked at a list and pushed a button. A young redheaded guard came in.

"Number 83," said the old man. "Don't forget to notify the kitchen."

"Yes, Sir!"

The redhead took him into a smaller room and frisked him.

"Follow me," said the guard.

Down a long hallway, up two flights of stairs. Another hallway, this one with cell doors on both sides. Another guard was standing at one of the doors peering through a peephole. He didn't even look up as they went by. A long, lazy yawn sounded from somewhere. They stopped before a door numbered 83, and the guard unlocked it. He motioned John inside with a clucking sound, as if he were giving a command to a dog. John took one step and the door closed on his heels. The reverberations shuddered through his whole body. He was at the end of the road. He slumped back against the door.

After a few seconds he noticed that there was another man in the cell. Lounging on a cot, he was busy with a string puzzle spanning the outstretched fingers of both hands.

"Look," he said, "that's called pig-in-a-pigpen!"

Then he stuffed the string into his pocket and stood up.

"I won't say welcome," he said with a half-grin. "But I must admit I'm glad to get some company. Let me introduce myself. I'm Van Doorn."

"John Van der Sloep," said John, holding out his hand. "At least, according to my I.D."

"Well, I'm Dirk Van Doorn, according to my I.D., birth certificate, wedding license, and diploma," said the other man. "I graduated from seminary as a missionary, but the war kept me here. You can call me Dirk. What crime have you committed?"

"I'm being held for questioning," said John, not quite sure how much to tell this man. "They'll probably be back for me in a few minutes."

"Then you'd better sit down and think through your story good and proper," said Dirk. "Whatever you tell them, stick to it! If you run into problems with your story, try it on me; maybe I can help. Want a drink of water?"

"Please!"

"Got anything in your pockets? Better let me have it. They'll search you again. Wait a minute. I'll get in front of the peephole. Now, sit down and concentrate on your story."

John sat at a little folding table jutting out from the wall for about half an hour before footsteps came echoing down the hall and stopped before the door. The small hatch in the door opened, and a hand shoved a tin into the cell.

"Two, if you please!" shouted Dirk. "I've got company today. And you can skip the wine and the steaks; we're both on a diet. Oh, hey, there's only one mattress in here. The second needn't be king size. A regular will do."

"Aye, aye, your majesty. Your every wish is my command," answered the guard from the other side of the door. The hatch fell shut.

"Oh boy, turnips!" said Dirk, bending over his little tin. "I love turnips."

John tried a bite, and his stomach revolted at the smell and texture of the food. Dirk eagerly accepted

John's portion and cleaned out both tins with his finger.

"You all set with your story?" he asked John.

"I guess so," he replied dispiritedly. What good would it do? Everything depended on Robert. If Robert failed, no story would save him. Sylvia would tell them all about him.

The time passed slowly. A guard came to bring John's mattress. Suddenly he realized that the long wait could be a good sign. They were going to bring her in to identify him. Why hadn't they done so?

A knock came from the next cell. Tap, tap, tap TAP. The "V" signal. Dirk tapped out a response. Then he lay down on the floor with his mouth next to the radiator pipe and spoke into it.

"A young fellow," he answered. "I don't know, I'm not his interrogator. Anything else? Invasion? You're nuts! I said, you're nuts! Hush!"

A loud thump on the door.

"Lights out!" someone shouted.

"Good night!" said Dirk. "You can relax now. They won't come to fetch you anymore tonight. You take the bed; I'll take the mattress on the floor. I insist! You're my guest, after all."

John stretched out on the bed. The blanket smelled like lysol. Where had he smelled that stench before? Westerbork, that's right, the camp at Westerbork! Out in the lush green grassland with . . . No, he mustn't think of that.

They lay talking in the dark until the guard came by for bed check.

Heavy boots clumped by. From down the hall came the sound of a bolt being slammed in place.

"Someone has been arrested," said Dirk. "You'll get used to it. Happens quite often. Sometimes in the middle of the night."

152

A soft tapping came from the neighbouring cell, but Dirk didn't respond. He told John about his wife and children, his voice sinking so low that John could barely hear him. He had a boy and a girl. He had never seen the girl. She had been born after he was picked up. He would have to wait until the end of the war. He hoped that he would be sent to a camp soon; then he would make it, he figured. If he stayed here, he was afraid that he would end up getting shot in a reprisal. Only a little while ago, twenty men had been lined up against the wall and murdered because somewhere a German soldier had been pushed into a canal.

"What are you in for?" asked John.

"Oh, the usual stuff: editing a little underground paper, helping some Jews. In short, I did everything I could to love God above all else and my neighbour as myself. Can't say I was always successful. I often failed. But it wasn't for my failures that they put me in jail." Then he added in a different voice. "Well, I bid you good night! Pleasant dreams. You have nothing to worry about: the doors are locked, the windows are closed, no thieves will bother you here. Sleep well, John!"

"Good night, Dirk."

Friends and brothers, although they had met but two hours ago. If only he didn't snore so loudly, thought John. Oh well, he had been told that he snored too. "I'll probably be awake all night," he said to himself.

A few minutes later, he dozed off. He awoke in the middle of the night thinking of Robert. A pale strip of moonlight slid across the floor from the window. Was he still waiting at the car? He thought of the others who had been put in a cell because of Sylvia. He prayed for them, but couldn't bring himself to mention her. Then he drifted off again.

As they washed themselves the next morning, the hatch popped open, and the face of a guard appeared in the small square.

"A new one?" said the square face. "Tell me, are you the one that shot the girl just three blocks down the street?"

"No," he said. "Is she dead?"

"Couldn't be deader. Three shots he pumped into her. I guess our lady killer's farther down."

The hatch banged shut. John grabbed Dirk by the arm.

"She's dead!" he whispered. "He did it! She's dead!"

"A traitor?"

"Yes. Dozens of lives depended on it."

"Then I'm glad for you."

"But they got my friend, the fellow that did it. He must be in this same wing. They got Robert!"

"God have mercy on him!" Dirk whispered gravely.

About ten o'clock the guard came for him. Dirk had given him some pointers. Lie without blushing! It's for a good cause. But lie intelligently and only when it is necessary. Swear if you have to. Don't deny anything too vehemently. Everything in the same tone of voice. If possible, confess to some minor thing; it might satisfy them. Don't be afraid of getting hit. After a while, you'll hardly feel it.

Behind a table sat three Germans. The middle one was a paunchy, gray-haired man, and on his left sat the man with the raspy voice who had picked John up. The fellow looked gaunt and ashen, but his eyes were hard and vicious.

The guard was dismissed. A soldier came into the room and stood right next to John. He was a husky young man with a thick neck and meaty hands.

John had to give his name. Then his place of residence, Meppel. No, he didn't speak German, but he could understand it a little.

"If you're from Meppel, what were you doing in Amsterdam?" asked the middle man.

John repeated what he had said the previous day. He was looking for his sister.

"The truth!" shouted his interrogator. The raspy-voiced man nodded at the soldier. Suddenly John was lying on the floor. The soldier's boots caught him in the hip and in the ribs, a big fist slammed into the side of his face, and then he was being yanked to his feet again.

"Get the idea? What were you doing in Amsterdam?"

"My sister," he said again and braced himself for another blow. He quivered with anger. In his mind's eye, he saw the soldier go sailing over the table. It would be so easy, but he had to restrain himself. He was only a boy from the country looking for his sister.

"What did you want your sister for?"

"I was fetching her. She ran away from home."

"So! And why did she run away?"

"She ran off with a German soldier. She's supposed to be in Amsterdam. I thought I saw her riding by."

"What's her name?"

"Tricia," he said. "Tricia Van der Sloep."

"You sure you're not making a mistake?"

"A mistake? No."

"Wasn't her name . . . Sylvia?"

"Wasn't," he had said. Past tense. So she *was* dead!

"No, my sister's name is Tricia."

The middle man sighed heavily, shrugged, looked at the raspy-voiced man, and went on.

"Were you a member of a hit squad?"

"A hit squad?"

The fat-faced German grinned.

"Yes," said the soldier next to him. "Hit, like this!"

Again John found himself on the floor. His whole cheek was numb. Still he managed to control himself.

"Now, listen," he said, standing groggily before the men at the table. He could hear that his voice was calm and cool. "You hit me one more time, and you don't get another word out of me. You can be sure of that! I always thought the Germans were civilized people. I've done nothing, and you'll have to let me go pretty soon. And then you can count on it, I know where to go to enter a complaint!"

That struck home, he noticed with satisfaction. The old one looked at raspy-voice and whispered something in his ear. Then he said to the soldier, "Get 594."

The soldier left. The three men behind the table sat back smoking. John stood waiting. His body throbbed in several spots, and every beat of his heart pounded in his head. Blood was running down his chin, but he didn't wipe it off. A pleasant tranquility settled on him, almost a sublime tranquility. He thought of the text that Grandpa Meyer had read, and which he had never really understood: "No weapon that is fashioned against you shall prosper . . ."

What a promise! What a wonderful promise from God! They could do whatever they liked, but they couldn't touch him. His self, his deepest self, they could never touch. Nor could they ever take this peace from him.

A sob of thankfulness welled up in his throat, a sob that turned into a laugh.

"What is it?" asked the fat interrogator.

John didn't answer. He couldn't explain it anyhow — maybe not to anyone, but surely not to this German.

The door opened. Someone was being dragged in between two soldiers. A confrontation? John noticed that the raspy-voiced man was keeping a sharp eye on him. So he fixed a deadpan expression on his face. He would recognize no one. And it was hard to recognize Robert in the battered, swollen creature that stood before him. But Robert straightened up, proud and aloof. His eyes, looking into John's, were as hard and cold as Sylvia's had ever been.

"Look at each other," the fat one said unnecessarily. "Do you know him?"

"No," said Robert. "Never seen him before."

"And you?"

"What about me?"

"You deaf? Do you *know* him?"

"Where am I supposed to know him from? This is the first time I've laid eyes on him."

"Take him away," said the German. Suddenly he banged on the table with his fist and screamed, "Get him out of here! You swine! Liars!"

Quickly they were shoved out into the hall, each by a different soldier. Then they were led back to the stairs in single file. Robert had difficulty walking, so John's guard prodded him past Robert. He glanced sideways. For a moment Robert's eyes met his; they passed over him and then stared straight ahead. No, they hadn't recognized each other. But each had greeted the other in his heart.

Dirk stood by the door waiting. He laid him down on the bed and washed his face gently. John laughed and wept.

"How'd it go?" asked Dirk.

"Great!" he said. "Say, do you know the verse, 'No weapon that is fashioned . . .'"

"Against you shall prosper."

"More!"

"And you shall confute every tongue that rises against you in judgment. Isaiah 54. I'll read it to you in a little while. I've got a little Bible with me."

They left him alone for three days. Then, once again, the guard came for him. He dreaded what was coming, and he prayed silently as he followed the guard down the corridor. This time the raspy-voiced man wasn't there. In his place was a uniformed stenographer, a broad-shouldered blonde who would have been pretty if she hadn't been so heavy. She had the hard eyes of a man. Nevertheless, the atmosphere was different, less hostile.

A photograph was thrown on the table in front of him.

"Do you know him?" Uncle Henry.

"No. Afraid not."

"How about him?" Pete.

"No. Him neither."

Then followed pictures of Angie and Aunt Nellie. No, no. All strangers. He didn't know any of them. It seemed to be going well.

Then came a large picture of Sylvia. That's how she had sat looking at him in the hospital — cool, imperial, with a slight smile that never reached her eyes.

He had hesitated.

"Ha, you know her!"

"No," he said calmly, "but she's very beautiful. I could look at her all day."

"She's not . . . your sister?"

"My sister? I should say not! My sister isn't near that pretty. She's just an average farm girl. Not that she's homely; she's a nice-looking girl. My mother told her . . ."

The man cut off his words by pushing another picture under his nose, face down.

"Take a good look! You know this one," he said with a grin, as if he had finally trapped John in a lie. He turned the picture over.

"Do you know him?"

John had just stopped himself from saying no. It was his own picture, as it had appeared in the police bulletin alongside Father's.

"Why, that's me!" he cried, as in surprise. In a flash he had realized two things: he couldn't very well deny knowing about this, but neither was it very serious. It sidetracked them from the original investigation.

The two men sat behind the table with triumphant smiles.

"You've lied to us!" said the other man in a high, reedy voice. It was the first time that John had heard him speak. Maybe he was self-conscious about his voice.

"Is your name John Van der Sloep?"

"No, John De Boer."

Then they extracted from him the whole story of the last day of the general strike, referring to the story in the police bulletin. But it provided them no rope to hang him with. He maintained that he had no idea why his picture had been put in the bulletin. Sure, his father had called a meeting at their home and, yes, that was illegal at the time. And his father had also taken in a pilot who had put up a fight after they fled. No, he hadn't turned himself in. But that was because he had been ducking the labour draft. He had finally given them a bone to chew on — but only a small one.

For the rest, he blamed Father. After all, he had been underage. This was a tactic everyone in the underground learned: once someone had been sentenced, blame everything on him. They never retried a man already sentenced. Besides, Father was in Dachau anyway.

"Where's your father?"

"I have no idea," he replied. "We think maybe he was shot some place."

He could go. No beating this time.

In the hall they met an official carrying a pile of papers. The man glanced at him, and then glanced again, sharply. It was the guard he had once contacted to smuggle messages to Father.

As his cell door closed behind him, and he began to speak to Dirk, there was a sudden commotion in the corridor, running and shouting, one German swearing loudly, and another one disclaiming responsibility.

Later that evening the news travelled along the pipes from cell to cell: a prisoner had committed suicide. He had jumped from the third floor stairwell. It was the man who had killed the girl.

That night John couldn't sleep. Again he saw the battered face and the cold, hard eyes so strikingly like Sylvia's. "Robert, Robert," he thought. "You were her last victim. And she got you more surely than she got anyone else."

Had he spoken out loud? For suddenly Dirk sat up and spoke.

"He didn't kill himself," he said. "They killed him just as surely as if they shot him. It was an act of self-preservation. Be glad he's out of his misery!"

The next day the cell door opened, and in stepped the official that John had seen in the hall the day before. He was a captain of the guard, John remembered. He carefully closed the door and held out his hand to John. He also seemed to know Dirk.

"Man," he said softly, "I couldn't believe my eyes when I suddenly saw you walking by. Did you hear? Your father was shipped to Germany. He was in good spirits when he went. Write a letter and I'll see it gets out. Be back in fifteen minutes. Don't put an address on it. I'll do it later."

With a little pencil stub supplied by Dirk, John quickly printed a note on a piece of toilet paper. He described his own case and mentioned Robert's death.

That was all. He ended by sending his love to Mother. He told the captain of the guard to deliver it to Dick Vriend. He would know how to get it to William.

A week later, he got William's reply. Aunt Nellie had been released. Because Sylvia could not testify against her, she was able to maintain that she was simply a landlady and had no idea what her boarders were up to. Angie had been moved to the prison camp at Vught, but plans had been laid to help her. Leo and William had joined another group, so the struggle went on.

A few days later, John was again taken from his cell and brought to another room. Behind a desk sat a young German, and in a corner, the strapping blonde stenographer. The man had a pleasant face.

"Good morning, I'm your caseworker," he said. "Gruber is my name."

The man was unusually amiable. He talked about love for one's country and his respect for the resistance. But, he said, at some point they had to face the fact that the game was over, if they were to retain their honour. They weren't really enemies, just opponents, so they had to behave like good sports. Didn't John agree? Yes, of course, completely!

Despite the camaraderie, John wasn't about to get trapped, and he stuck to everything that he had said earlier. The man didn't seem to be very well informed about his case, for he kept putting on his glasses to look at the dossier. Finally, heaving a big sigh, he tossed the dossier into a drawer and stood up.

"I don't want to tire you," he said, with affected concern. "We'll talk more tomorrow. But then there will be some changes, my young friend. You will begin telling me the truth. I am getting tired of these adolescent games. Your only chance is to be absolutely honest with me. *Auf Wiedersehen.*"

As he was talking, he pressed a button. The guard entered and led John back to his cell. There, Dirk warned John several times, looking anxious.

"Watch out, John! He may appear easygoing, but this man is more dangerous than the others. Once he has worked himself into your dossier, he'll trap you on a single word, or on the tone of your voice."

But the interview didn't resume until three days later. Gruber politely apologized for not getting back to him sooner. He had taken a couple of days off, he explained. Someone had been taking a car to Osnabruck, his hometown, and he hadn't been able to resist the temptation to ride along.

Had John ever been there? No, never. He should. After the war. He'd like it. And then they had drifted into a long talk about John's home province, Drenthe, comparing it to the country around Osnabruck. For a while John forgot why he was here. He was saved only by the lingering force of Dirk's warning. Watch out! Had he unknowingly given something away?

"About your case. You know that redheaded friend of yours, William. Is that his name?"

But John didn't bite. What was that? A redhead? No, he didn't remember any redhead by that name. No, his father had given shelter only to a pilot, and he was no redhead. Besides, the fellow had died in the fire, or so he had been told.

For an hour the man drilled him about William and Pete, and then Sylvia and Angie. He stifled his jubilation as he saw frustration growing in his interrogator's eyes. "I've got him checkmated," thought John.

The door opened, and another officer put his head around the corner.

"You still at it?" asked his colleague. "Did you forget? The champagne is already on ice."

162

Throwing the dossier back into the drawer, Gruber jumped up and headed for the door. He stopped with his hand on the knob.

"The stenographer will call a guard to take you back to your cell when she is finished," he said. "*Auf Wiedersehen.*"

He was gone. The stenographer did as her boss had ordered. First she finished what she was doing and tidied up, and then she rang for the guard. She gave John a bold, scornful stare as she walked out, as if to show him that she wasn't the slightest bit afraid to be alone with him.

He hadn't planned to do it; he was moving before he had thought it through. As soon as the blonde woman had closed the door behind her, he darted to the other side of the desk, pulled open the second drawer on the left, and grabbed his dossier. As he sank back into his chair, it was already tucked securely under his shirt. Only then did his pulse begin to race. The big portrait of Hitler on the wall had seen nothing. And he had all of ten seconds to compose himself before the door opened.

Feigning nonchalance, he slowly got up and followed the guard. Actually, he felt like doing cartwheels down the corridor. When he got back to the cell, he hugged Dirk. While Dirk stood in front of the peephole, John quickly read everything in his dossier. Gruber was out drinking champagne anyway. In the file was everything that Sylvia and the others had said about him. Angie hadn't said a thing, but Louis had spilled everything he knew. There wasn't a word in it about the shooting on the Yssel Bridge. Not that this surprised him. Otherwise they would surely have asked him about it. But how had Sylvia neglected to mention the thing that had put him in the hospital for so many months?

The immediate problem, however, was what to do with the dossier.

"Eat it," said Dirk. "Give me a few sheets. I love paper! It's like cherry pie without the cherries."

"No, you better lay off," said John. "My stomach is in a lot better shape than yours. You can have my leftovers."

It wasn't at all like cherry pie, but he forced everything down that contained information which might be harmful to him. The rest he tossed straight into the slop pail. He had a terrific bellyache that night, but he comforted himself with the knowledge of what he had accomplished.

After this, John was left alone. The Germans worked systematically, keeping everything in dossiers and card files. Only those cases recorded on paper came up for attention, so John's case was forgotten. Despite his display of concern, Gruber, too, had apparently forgotten him.

The days were growing longer and the sun was warmer. Sometimes they took off their shirts and took turns standing in a narrow strip of sunshine to help maintain their health and strength. This was one of Dirk's central concerns. He never skipped his morning exercises, either.

In early May, Dirk was suddenly put on a transport to Germany. He was in high spirits when he left, and he willed all his possessions to John — the pencil stub, a razor blade that he used by inserting it between the tines of a fork, and his piece of string with all his tricks written down on a piece of paper. They had grown very fond of each other, but they covered up the pain of parting with jokes and laughter. They promised to look each other up after the war and vowed to maintain their friendship for the rest of their lives.

That evening two tins of food were slid through the hatch as usual. Apparently Dirk's name hadn't yet been scratched off the kitchen list. But John held his tongue. He had gotten over his queasiness about prison food. With the meagre prison diet, he was thankful for the extra portion. Turnips! By now he liked turnips almost as much as Dirk did. He licked out both tins.

He missed Dirk. They had played checkers together, prayed together, and washed one another's backs. However, he had also showed John how to survive on his own. A veteran jailbird, he could communicate with other prisoners along the radiator and water pipes. He was able to assess the rumours that were passed from cell to cell. There was constant talk of the invasion; invasion fever was rampant even inside the prison. With his fork, John bored a small hole beside the hatch so that he could look out into the corridor. This provided him many hours of diversion.

What had been Dirk's greatest fear was now his — reprisals. Although his dossier had been destroyed, his name was still in the prison card file. Would he, too, be sent to a German camp one of these days? Or would the invasion finally come this year?

A couple of chickadees were building a nest somewhere on the prison grounds. He couldn't see exactly where, but the birds flew back and forth past his cell window all day long carrying feathers and straw.

"When the baby birds arrive," he told himself, "the invasion will come."

A couple of weeks later, the two chickadees were flying by with insects and worms. The babies had hatched! But there was no sign of an invasion. Meanwhile, a black market dealer had been put in the cell with him. His new cellmate was an irritable man who acted as if he owned the place. But he didn't stay very long. He was replaced by a young fellow, even younger than John, who had been arrested for illegal activities, that is, for helping the underground. Now John was the veteran who could help and comfort the new-comer, as Dirk had once done for him.

The chickadees were no longer flying by. The young ones had already flown off on their own. On the sixth or seventh of June — he had lost track of the exact date — the news travelled along the pipes that the Allies had arrived in Rome. That same night came the news that the invasion had finally been launched. As an experienced sifter of prison rumours, John concluded that the first was probably true and that the latter was no doubt just another rumour.

After lights out, the cell door was suddenly thrown open and the light switched on. In the door stood a strange German in regular army uniform, a grenade dangling from his belt and the insignia of the S.S. on his sleeve. In his hand he carried a list of names.

"De Boer?"

"Yes?"

"Come along. Take all your clothes. Move!"

"Transport?" asked John.

"Just move!" repeated the soldier. "You've got five minutes."

John was dressed in a flash. Transport! The concentration camp. It was frightening but also exciting — fear mingled with hope and expectation. He would feel fresh air, see the night sky, maybe people on the street. He looked at his cellmate. He was still sleeping. He could sleep through anything! But he was a good fellow, and he wasn't in on very serious charges. He should make it without too much trouble. John let him sleep, putting the pencil stub and the string on the little folding table along the wall. The razor blade had finally broken.

Goodbye, cell! Strange, he had almost grown attached to the small, barren space. Here was the soldier again. About twenty men had been mustered in the corridor. A murmur rippled along the row.

"Silence!"

John was at the end of the line, beside an old man wearing a cap on his bandaged head. In front of the prison stood a canvas-covered truck. They were herded aboard with a minimum of words and a generous helping of kicks and blows. The tailgate of the truck was high, and John stopped to give the old man a boost. He in turn got a boost from one of the soldiers — with the toe of his boot.

He slid to the end of the bench nearest the back of the truck, where he would be able to enjoy the fresh air. A German soldier jumped onto the truck and elbowed John over into the old man to make plenty of room for himself. Grumbling, the whole row slid down for them. Another German took the end seat on the opposite bench. Then a third crawled over the tailgate and, swearing and kicking at their legs, made his way to the back of the cab, where he sat between the two rows of prisoners and facing the open end of the truck. There were five soldiers but two rode up front with the driver.

They began moving out of the city. John knew Amsterdam well, and he recognized every turn and street. When they crossed the Berlage Bridge, he knew that they were heading for Amersfoort — not very good news! It was a rough camp, even worse than Vught.

The soldier next to him coughed and spat over the tailgate. What time was it? Were his eyes deceiving him, or was the eastern horizon beginning to pale? Would they see the sunrise? He laughed at himself — excited about seeing a sunrise!

The truck roared along the rough road, and the big German's body rocked with every bump. The man rested his arms and chin on the butt of his rifle, which he had propped between his knees. The cold morning air gusted into the back of the truck. John shivered.

When they arrived in Amersfoort, it was still quite dark. They drove through town, hardly slowing down.

A murmur went up from the prisoners. The truck had not turned into the road leading to the camp!

"Silence!" shouted the soldier sitting against the cab, pounding his rifle butt on the floor of the truck. And everyone was quiet again.

Now they took a road leading into the sparsely populated area of the Veluwe. Soon there was rugged countryside on both sides. Where were they going? They couldn't very well take them all the way to Germany by truck, could they? But then why were they being taken out here into this deserted countryside? For execution?

John's heart contracted with fear. They couldn't do that! That wasn't fair! He hadn't even been tried! Besides, his wasn't a serious case. Even Dirk had thought that he would be released soon. Panic made his breath come faster. He tried to study the faces of the other prisoners, but it was still too dark. They were whispering. He sensed that they had come to the same conclusion as he.

"One of us must survive . . ." Father was in a German concentration camp. Maybe he would never come back. In fact, it would be a miracle if he did. So he, John, *had* to survive. He had to take care of Mother and the children.

Should he? What kind of chance did he have? Out of the corner of his eye, he studied the soldier beside him. Slouched over his rifle butt, he seemed to be asleep. The face of the soldier across from him was shrouded in the shadow of the truck canopy, but he was sprawled back in his corner.

How fast was the truck going? Forty . . . fifty kilometres per hour? He could break his neck! He might as well admit it: he was afraid! Yet, what could he lose? To die now or an hour from now — what was the difference?

He gathered his feet under the bench, all his muscles coiled and tense. He leaned forward slightly to

168

look out of the end of the truck. In the faint glimmer of early dawn, he could just make out the shapes of trees, and beyond, the dark shadow of a forest. What was he waiting for? This was an ideal spot. Roll with the truck and protect your head, he told himself. He could move fast; he had learned how to fall. His judo lessons would come in handy. As he jumped, he would have to turn so that he rolled forward. What else could he do? Why hesitate?

"God give me strength, give me courage," he prayed. "Bring one of us home." Then he was leaping past the soldier, and as he jumped, he knew that he had timed it right. His feet hit the road and he tumbled forward, rolling over and over behind the truck.

Then he lay still. He was conscious. He hurt all over, but he could stand up. Nothing was broken! He began running away from the road. A ditch tripped him up, and he fell forward into the water. He scrambled up, and then he was in the trees — pine trees. Not until then did he hear a shot and tires skidding.

But he was already well into the trees; the woods swallowed him up into their merciful darkness. More shots, but none hit anywhere near him. He ran into some dense scrub wood that almost stopped him, catching at his clothes. Then he remembered a childhood trick: dropping to his hands and knees, he began crawling along the rabbit trails. For a strange, confusing moment, he was playing with his brother in the shrubbery near his childhood home. Then he heard voices behind him, not the voices of children but of German soldiers. More shooting. Maybe the other prisoners were also making a run for it!

Suddenly he was out of the trees. He ran, stumbling and tripping, over a ploughed field. His legs and wind were giving out. He had been locked up too long. Another ditch! He didn't have the strength to try to jump it, so he lumbered into the water and waded across. The water revived him a little. He plodded on across one field and into another, sinking deep into ploughed soil, putting himself between the strands of one barbed wire fence after another.

After staggering across yet another field of young oats, he reached the bank of a small canal and collapsed into the grass, his heart beating as if it would burst. He couldn't take another step.

But as he lay there looking up at the sky, panting, the smell of the earth, of the grass, and of the young crop filled him with a gladness that he hadn't known for a long time. He pulled out a handful of the tall, lush grass and held it to his nose. He picked a stalk of sorrel grass from the handful, put it in his mouth and chewed on it, as he had done when he was a young boy in Drenthe. Drenthe! Where Mother waited. He was still alive. He had survived! He was free again. One of us must survive!

Three cows stood on the other bank of the canal staring at him, their heads lowered over the water. Someone was coming across the pasture! John lowered himself into the canal and pulled himself along the bank, but the cows followed him, snorting and blowing. The man was calling them, "Hoyo, hoyo! Here, girl," in a sing-song chant, as every Saxon farmer calls his cows. He caught up to his cows and stood in the grass on the water's edge looking down at John.

"What in the world are you doing in there?" he asked in surprise. "Who *are* you?"

The man seemed more amused than alarmed. John tried to climb up the bank, but he couldn't summon the strength. The man seized his hand and pulled him up.

"Ah, now I see! Running from the Germans, eh? Ai-yai-yai, man! What did they do to you? You're covered with blood!"

"The truck . . ." gasped John. "I jumped . . . from the truck . . . They were trying to shoot me!"

"They didn't hit you, did they?" the man asked anxiously, looking him up and down. "I think I heard the gunfire! Just before I came out to do the milking, I said to my wife, 'Why, that sounds like shots!' Well, you come with me. My wife can fix you up. The cows will just have to wait a bit."

He took John by the arm and helped him across the pasture, the cows following right on their heels. They passed through a gate and crossed a dirt road skirting dense woods. Birds twittered and chirped, and a curlew rose out of the trees, singing jubilantly. The man chatted on. How wonderful to hear an ordinary human being talking about regular, everyday things. But he also talked about the war.

"Yes," he said, "it will sure be a relief when this miserable war is over! But like I was saying to my wife, it shouldn't last much longer, now that the invasion has come!"

"What?" John stopped. "The invasion? When? Where?"

"Oh, they started landing about a day or so ago, I guess," said the farmer. "Some place in France. What did they call it again? Normandy! That's in France, isn't it? My boy's teacher says the Allies lost a lot of men, but they're gradually pushing the Germans back."

The invasion! Finally, the real thing. They'd *better* be pushing the Germans back! All those years of waiting, the promises, the preparations. Were their trials finally coming to an end? The new day! Finally, the new day was going to come!

They came out of the woods. The farmer stopped.

"There's my farm," he said, pointing. "And will you look at that!"

On the horizon behind his farm, the sky was awash with orange from one end to the other. At the centre, where the sun would soon appear, was a brilliant glow. The sun still lay behind the horizon, but the sky was luminous with the promise of its coming. The countryside seemed to be holding its breath in anticipation.

No one could stop the course of the sun, and no one could stop the course of God's justice — not even Hitler.

The Story of a Poor Scholar by Deborah Alcock
A Story about Germany and Bohemia

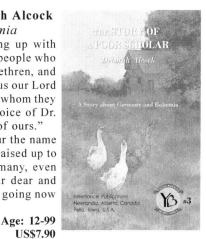

"Indeed?" said the old man, his face lighting up with sympathy and interest. "We have heard of the people who are called Brethren of the Unity, or United Brethren, and we own them as brethren indeed, in Christ Jesus our Lord — whose Gospel they knew and honoured, and whom they served and died for, many years before the voice of Dr. Martin Luther was heard in this Saxon land of ours."

"And we also," Wenzel responded, "we honour the name of your great teacher, Dr. Luther, whom God raised up to show His pure Evangel to the people of Germany, even as, one hundred years before, He sent us our dear and venerated Master John Huss. That is why I am going now to Wittenberg, to pursue my studies there."

Time: 1550s	**Age: 12-99**
ISBN 978-1-928136-96-5	**US$7.90**

The Martyr of Kolin by H.O. Ward
A Story of the Bohemian Persecution

When I reached home from afternoon school, I went up to a little upper chamber which Wilma and I had as our own, and there I found my sister — who was at the time a fair young maiden of thirteen — busy with her needle.

"Well, Sister," said I, "so we are to have another of these good gentlemen tonight."

"He has come," she said mysteriously.

"Has he? What is he like?" I asked.

"I have not seen him, for he is closeted with our father in his private chamber."

"Will he sup openly with us tonight?"

"Yes, I think so. Elspeth will keep a careful watch, and there is the door behind the tapestry, you know, in case of a surprise."

Time: 1560-1580	**Age: 12-99**
ISBN 978-1-928136-47-7	**US$12.90**

The Martyr's Widow by Deborah Alcock
A Story About The Netherlands

"Flee, Carl! Oh, flee while you can!"

"It is too late! Where should I flee to?"

Another loud impatient knock, and a sound of rough voices outside.

But a thought, sent as she believed from Heaven into her heart, inspired Lisa with sudden hope and courage. She seized her husband by the arm, and drew him toward the little closet, the door of which she had left open.

"There — in there — fear nothing — I will speak to them."

Time: 1570s	**Age: 12-99**
ISBN 978-1-77298-000-4	**US$7.90**

Robert Musgrave's Adventure
by Deborah Alcock
A Story of Old Geneva

"Josef . . . the servant, ye know," said Jeannot, "told us how the soldiers of Captain Brunaulieu's corps, as they came to a halt outside the town, found amongst them a boy who was evidently a Genevan. They seized him, and brought him to the Captain. He said he was an Englishman, which, I suppose, is another kind of heretic . . . oh, I crave pardon of your Worthinesses . . ."

"Never mind our Worthinesses, but go on with thy story," said someone.

"The Captain would have had him run through at once. But the holy Friar who was with them — Friar Alexander the Scotchman, they called him — bade spare him, as he might be of use in the town for a guide. 'Twas just then that Josef, who told us the tale, came up, being sent on a message . . ."

Time: 1602   Age: 12-99
ISBN 978-1-928136-32-3   US$8.90

Sunset in Provence by Deborah Alcock
A Tale of the Albigenses

"My lord, I am your sister's son but not your vassal," the youth replied with perhaps unnecessary pride. "But that is not the question," he added sadly and in a gentler tone. "You counsel me — no, you command me," and he bowed his head slightly at the word, "to submit myself unreservedly to our Holy Father the Pope, in the person of his Legate."

"I do, as you do value life and lands. If your retainers had not infected you with their heresy, why should you hesitate?"

"I — the son of Roger Taillefer — a heretic! None of our race were ever that, thank Heaven. But can the Count ask why I hesitate? Not that I fear the disgrace of a public penance, though I think they might have spared it to the greatest seigneur who speaks the 'Langue d'Oc', and altogether such a submissive and obedient Roman Catholic."

Time: 1200s   Age: 12-99
ISBN 978-1-928136-94-1   US$7.90

The Cloak in Pledge by Deborah Alcock
A Story About Russia

"If we only had something better for the little one," Ivan added, in a lower tone. "He can't eat that."

"Don't fret, Father," said Michael, a good-humoured lad on the whole. "I'll ask Master to give me a roll for him at dinner-time, and besides, there's Peter —" (the brother next in age, who had just got a place as one of the boy-postillions the wealthy Russians were so fond of having) — "Peter may come and see us, and bring us a kopeck or two for him."

Time: 1800s   Age: 12-99
ISBN 978-1-928136-95-8   US$7.90

Archie's Chances by Deborah Alcock
A Story of the Nineteenth Century

This was scarcely as bad as she expected, yet quite bad enough. She flushed hotly. "Uncle has not said anything to you, has he?" she asked.

"Never once. Kate, Uncle Morris is a brick!" There was a wealth of genuine gratitude flung into the boyish word that redeemed it from all trace of vulgarity.

"If Father were alive, what would he say?" questioned Kate. "I think he would be horrified at the very thought."

"Well, I don't know," mused Archie, thrusting his hands into his pockets. "After all, the horrible thing is eating the shop — I mean the bread that's made in it. And since I do that already, and can't help myself, I think it would not make things any worse to earn it before I eat it."

Time: 1880s   **Age: 12-99**
ISBN 978-1-894666-16-9   **US$8.90**

Truth Stranger Than Fiction by Deborah Alcock
The King of Hungary's Blacksmith
and other Stories

"Well, Master Jailer, how goes it? Have you heard anything?" asked the young man in an eager whisper.

The jailer laid his hand compassionately on his shoulder. "Heavy tidings for thee, poor lad," he said. "He will likely die."

The answer was a deep groan, heard distinctly through all the uproar of the crowded room. Then silence; then a broken murmur, "Poor Maida — poor baby!" choked by something very like the suppressed sob of a strong man.

Time: 1570s   **Age: 12-99**
ISBN 978-1-77298-001-1   **US$7.90**

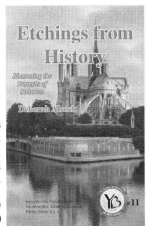

Etchings from History by Deborah Alcock
Illustrating the Proverbs of Solomon

After a brief though brilliant career (in which he rendered important political services to the cause of Protestantism), Maurice was killed in the battle of Sievershausen, in his thirty-second year. He had enjoyed his electorate about five years. His brother succeeded him, for his only son had died before him. One little daughter, Anna, survived him. She was afterward married, with great pomp and show, to the celebrated William the Silent, Prince of Orange.

Time: 1570s   **Age: 12-99**
ISBN 978-1-928136-97-2   **US$7.90**

The Reformation Trail Series

RT01 *Hubert Ellerdale* by W. Oak Rhind
A Tale of the Days of Wycliffe

Christine Farenhorst in *Christian Renewal*: Christians often tend to look on the Reformation as the pivotal turning point in history during which the Protestants took off the chains of Rome. This small work of fiction draws back the curtains of history a bit further than Luther's theses. Wycliffe was the morning star of the Reformation and his band of Lollards a band of faithful men who were persecuted because they spoke out against salvation by works. Hubert Ellerdale was such a man and his life (youth, marriage, and death), albeit fiction, is set parallel to Wycliffe's and Purvey's. Rhind writes with pathos and the reader can readily identify with his lead characters. This novel deserves a well-dusted place in a home, school, or church library.

Time: 1380-1420	Age: 13-99
ISBN 0-921100-09-4	US$12.95

RT02 *Crushed Yet Conquering*
by Deborah Alcock
A Story of Constance and Bohemia

A gripping story filled with accurate historical facts about John Huss and the Hussite wars. **Hardly any historical novel can be more captivating and edifying than this book.** Even if Deborah Alcock was not the greatest of nineteenth century authors, certainly she is our most favourite.
— Roelof & Theresa Janssen

Time: 1414-1436	Age: 11-99
ISBN 1-894666-01-1	US$19.95

RT03 *The Roman Students* by Deborah Alcock
A Tale of the Renaissance

Raymond felt the force of the last argument. Besides, he could not contend the point; his schoolfellow had him in his power. A little water

from the crystal flask that lay on the table, a fine white kerchief from the looms of Cambray, and a pair of gentle, firm, skilful hands soon accomplished the task. Theodore's words sometimes missed their aim, and hurt where they meant to heal, his fingers never. Their very form — long, slender, sensitive — evidenced at once fineness of perception and exquisite dexterity.

Meanwhile the schoolfellows talked of the unfair and dastardly conduct of the Nicoloti, and formed plans of revenge. What they said was commonplace enough, but they speedily established a friendly understanding with each other.

"I had not known you were destined to be a physician," said Raymond. "Is not that to sacrifice your genius and your learning?"

Time: 1440s	Age: 15-99
ISBN 978-1-928136-93-4	US$17.90